Justified by Law and Conflict

—A NOVEL—

SPENCER LENNARD SMITH

Justified by Law and Conflict

Spencer Lennard Smith

JUSTIFIED BY LAW AND CONFLICT

First printing: January 2021
Printed in the United States of America
Published by:
Editor: Executive Business Writing
Cover Designer & Photographer: Reginald H. Blair

Table of Contents

Special Acknowledgement

I would like to acknowledge Mr. Reginald H. Blair for his professional work and expertise as the Cover Designer & Photographer.

Dedication

This book is dedicated to Irene B. Jones, Robert L. Smith, Karen Smith, Spencer Smith, Jr., Makita B. Johnson, Sabre L. Smith, Christopher Johnson, Cedric Allum, Floyd Whitfield, Dorothy Whitfield, Lloyd Whitfield, Minda Potts, Millicent Hill, William Hill, Angela Hill, Melody Armstead, Lloyd Armstead, and certainly to all of my family and friends.

Introduction

As children, we are taught to respect our parents, our elders, leaders in the community, and certainly those in law enforcement. I came up during a time when not only could your parents correct and discipline you, but the neighbors could do so as well. It was a time of love, pride, and respect.

My mother raised me to be honest, trustworthy, and loyal to my friends and family members. As I entered into my pre-adult years, I began to be exposed to things that didn't necessarily line up with all that had been instilled in me.

My first writing, "To Help Push and Pull Me Through," was instrumental in opening the door of the gift of storytelling in hopes of garnering an audience that understands the many atrocities of being a minority. Whether African American, Hispanic, Asian, or other, we've all experienced racism by those who were sworn to serve and protect us.

Perhaps you will find yourself or someone you know within the pages of this novel. In any event, if you see something, say something.

Introduction

Chapter 1

My Father

It's called the City of Angels. It sits right near the southern part of the golden state of California. It has some of the best weather you could ever ask for. During the early 1950's many African Americans were making an exodus from the racist Jim Crow South, where Jim Crow laws justified white citizens in conflicts with Black citizens in the South. My parents, Mary Bell Smith and Robert Smith, Sr., were a part of that exodus. California was promising to African Americans. Within a few weeks of coming to California, my father was fortunate to land a good paying job. As a colored man, he became a peace officer, patrolling the city streets of Los Angeles. He was a tall, proud, and handsome young 32-year-old man with a heavy southern drawl. He was dedicated to his wife and job as an officer.

My mother was a young, adorable homemaker and mother-to-be. They settled down in a small one-bedroom, storefront apartment. A spiral staircase would lead you to the front door. Their rooms had shiny wood grain floors throughout, with white marble counter tops in the kitchen. The cabinet doors in the kitchen were mahogany wood. Their first home was located on 42nd Street and Central Avenue. It was the colored section of Los Angeles, near the famous Dunbar Hotel. The Dunbar also served as a nightclub. Well-known colored entertainers and other noteworthy colored people would go there to enjoy themselves without discrimination. It was a place where colored people looked out or each other and made sure to protect one another. A typical morning conversation between my parents would take place with my Dad teasing my Mom.

"Good morning! Oh, what's that cooking, good looking? It smells so good! Is there enough for me?"

"Good morning, honey! Yes! You know that's my smothered potatoes, eggs, and gravy."

"Yeah, I can't wait to get my share, so come on with it! I'll take mines right now, let me get my plate!"

"Hold on! Hold on, babe! It's not quite done yet!" she smiled.

"All right, dear. Hey what do you think about going out dancing and finger popping tonight when I get home?"

"Yeah, but you're going to have to take it easy on me on the dance floor; I don't want to have this baby on the dance floor."

"I don't want you to have my baby on the dance floor, either!"

"Okay! But do you have your dancing shoes ready?"

"I keep my shoes ready, babe!" (My father laughed).

"Okay, I'll be ready when you get home."

My father loved joking and playing around the house with my mother. They would always joke with each other. They kept a romantic atmosphere in and outside of the home. They would share a kiss whenever they encountered each other, especially when my father would approach my mother in the kitchen. As a young couple, they were very much in love. My father would get up two hours early in order to prepare his uniform and polish his shoes for work. He loved enthusiastically sharing his daily work experiences with my mother. My mother would just stand back and take in an earful of information, listening attentively, all the while cooking one of her special dishes in the kitchen, wearing an apron over her neatly ironed flowered dress.

By this time, November 17, 1964, my mother was six months pregnant. My father's duties were to patrol the seedy section of Hollywood, California. Hollywood is where all the best motion pictures were made for the entire world to see, and where you could see all the big movie stars' names in neon lights and their names on stars engraved in the concrete sidewalks. You could also see ladies of the night working the streets as prostitutes, heroin junkies creeping around corners on just about every corner, big money pimps and dope dealers promising to sell you a dream of a lifetime, and even businessmen scheming with white-collar crimes also hung out there. Those were common citizens with devious intent, willing to do something wrong or illegal.

During one of his late-night routes, my father, Robert, and his partner, Frank, who was white, received a call that stated that a pawnshop burglary was in progress.

"Robbery in progress at Hollywood and Vine," the dispatcher's voice droned across the police car radio.

"Come on, Frank, let's roll." My father pushed his foot to the pedal and sped down the street, without his siren blaring.

As they approached the address of the building, the alarm was a loud, blaring noise. They parked the squad car, and as soon as their feet hit the pavement, there was somewhat of an ambush, as without warning, they were fired upon.

Officer Frank shouted out, "Robert! I'm hit! I can't breathe!" Frank grabbed his chest as he collapsed.

Officer Robert yelled into his walkie with a loud, but rapidly weakening voice. "Radio to headquarters! Radio to headquarters! Officers need help! Officers need help! Frank! Frank! I'm hit, too! Oh, my God! Frank! Talk to me, Frank! Frank! Headquarters! Headquarters come in! Officers down! Oh my God! Oh my God! Frank!

"This is headquarters. Talk to me!" the voice crackled back over the radio.

"Yeah, this is Officer Smith. I've been shot! I've been shot! My partner is down too! We're at 4512 West Hollywood Boulevard! Shots fired! Officers down! Officers down!"

The dispatch replied, "We're sending all units! I repeat! We're sending all units!"

They didn't stand a chance. Their bullet-riddled bodies lay sprawled out in pools of blood on the street and sidewalk amongst the stars that were engraved in the concrete sidewalks at the corner of Hollywood Boulevard and Vine Street.

The investigation discovered that there was no burglary break in, just a broken window that sounded the alarm to the building. It was a very dark location. There was no one on the scene, no witnesses, no assailants, just Officers Frank McElroy and Robert Smith, dead on the spot.

The homicide detectives labeled it as a cold case file, an unsolved criminal investigation, still open pending the discovery of new evidence today, though no one was ever apprehended. Talk was around town that a local street pimp name Sweet Rudy had made a connection to the streets from his prison cell. He paid $2,000.00 for and ordered a hit on my father and his partner, Officer McElroy.

My Father

Sweet Rudy had transported young girls from state to state. My father and his partner had arrested him for prostituting underage girls. He had been sentenced and sent to prison. The richest of the white businessmen in Hollywood were his clientele until my father and his partner took Sweet Rudy down. Rumor had it that half of the $2,000.00 was put up by some of those businessmen.

Just months away from delivering me, my mother had the burden of burying my father in a peace officer's memorial. He was one of the first officers from the Los Angeles Department to be killed in the line of duty in 20 years. His casket was driven by horse and carriage. The procession led throughout the streets of downtown Los Angeles with the funeral held at True Grace Missionary Baptist Church. After, they proceeded to Forest Lawn Memorial Park Cemetery where his body went to its final resting place.

On February 12, 1965, my mother delivered me. She had relocated to 11661 S. Avalon Boulevard, Apt. #2, a two-bedroom wall-to-wall green shag carpet apartment with linoleum flooring and white painted cabinet doors in the kitchen. The cross street was 116th street, which some would say was smack-dab in the heart of south-central Los Angeles, a predominantly African American and Latino section of the city. It wasn't until I began kindergarten and noticed some of my fellow students had fathers, that I began asking my mother about my father. She would tell me short stories about my father as I journeyed through my grade school years.

"Momma, I've seen Earl and Tyrone's dads waiting on them, sitting in their cars, and picking them up from school. I often wonder about Dad, what do you remember most about him? I need to know more about him."

"My favorite memory is his smile and his godliness, and just being a great man, with a sense of humor. He was a Christian, a loving man who cared about everyone. He made everything better, even on a bad day. The fact that he was protecting and serving, this is the way, I feel in my heart of hearts, that he would have liked to leave this earth. Like I've always told you, your daddy couldn't wait to see you. He often spoke about you becoming a young hero for our people. He wanted you to be like Dr. Martin Luther King, Jr., or even a Malcolm X. He had a lot of plans for you, once we found out we were having a boy."

My mother and I lived on the small pension of a deceased Los Angeles police officer as she worked part-time as a teacher's aide at my old elementary school, 116th Street School, to supplement the household income. She drove a 1973 sky blue Chevy Impala. My mother would call me little Robert, Jr. when I was around the house, but when we were in public, she'd just keep it at Robert. And in return I would call her "Momma," although her name was Mary Bell Smith.

My mother was one of the most beautiful women I've ever seen, inside and out. She was always a very neat dresser with well-kept hair. She was the kindest person I'd ever met. However, she would sometimes use a few swear words when she would chastise and reprimand me. I would respond in kind. I guess without an older man in the house, I would try to put her through the test. She would always pass that test by handing out an ass whipping to me, up until I was done testing her.

I loved and feared my mother. I had a great deal of respect for older Black men as well. When I would see older Black men, I would sometimes reflect and imagine my father. But I understood that my mother was my protector, and she managed to receive and keep my father's .38 special service revolver, as she strongly believed in God and the gun.

Momma and I would often attend our neighborhood church. She influenced me to believe in God and protect and defend myself in the community. She would always want to see me to do better in whatever I was doing. She'd often remind me of how much I looked like my daddy while wearing a grin on her face in the process, I would often observe her compassion toward our neighbors, especially when a neighbor was in need of something. She would sometimes sacrifice her time to go to a needy neighbor to see if there was something she could do. She would cook southern dinners like her mother had cooked for her back in Shreveport, Louisiana, which is where she and my father were born and raised before coming to California.

By the early 1980's we were still part of an African American community that was just getting by on the bare-minimum, and my education was just the same. I maneuvered through the mean streets of south-central Los Angeles, and although I was not in a gang, I had associates and cousins who were gang affiliated. That made me guilty by association, according to the Los Angeles police. All of the police were coming down hard on the gang members. I believed they thought gang members didn't have fathers at home to keep them out of trouble. They felt that they would play the strict disciplinary role on the streets. I didn't get involved with the gang activity. My mother was the chairperson of the local Neighborhood Watch committee. She always tried to guide me in the opposite direction of the ills in the big city. Therefore, she constantly lectured me on daily activities and current events.

"Son, I've been watching some of your cousins and these boys around here in that gang stuff. I want you to stay clear of that behavior. Can't anything good come out of that, you hear?"

"Mom, they don't mean any harm! I've known those guys since I was born! They're cool."

"Yeah, maybe not! But you heard what I said? I'm trying to keep you out of trouble."

"Yeah! I heard you mom! Those guys are some real cool dudes."

"A lot of the problems they have are full of misunderstanding riffs, jealousy and envy and that can lead to death."

"I don't have a problem with those guys. They just like running games on people, that's all."

"I want you to grow up and become a good man, and men don't play games that bring about a misunderstanding!"

"All right!"

A lot of the guys considered me a square because I didn't indulge in any of the weed smoking and beer drinking in high school. But the girls were always on my main menu. Unfortunately, I wasn't too appealing to a lot of the fine young girls due to my overweight problem and other issues. I was a seventeen-and-a-half-year-old dark-skinned Black kid (a negative in those days), wearing bifocals with a dry ass Jeri curl, weighing around about 190 pounds. I stood at 5'9," along with a face full of sporadic acne. I loved to listen to hip-hop and rhythm and blues music on my Walkman earphones.

I attended Locke High School, which was located on 111th and San Pedro Street. It wasn't quite a mile from my apartment, although between Locke High School and our apartment was the intersection of Imperial Highway and Avalon, and that's where anything goes. We had some of the best hamburger and fried chicken stands, and an arcade. There was alcohol, weed, and cheap motel rooms with sex being sold. You could stand there on that corner and witness a little bit of everything.

"Li'l Robert, you really need to be careful going and coming from school, because I'm hearing a lot of police activity up there on that intersection! You hear me?"

I had to let her know I could handle myself.

"Yeah, Mom. I'm watching my back when I walk through that intersection."

"Okay!"

"You don't have to worry, Mom! I'm good!"

"Boy! I'm not asking you if you are good! I'm telling you to be careful and watch your ass out there!"

"Okay, okay I got you!"

It was a section of Los Angeles where you really needed to keep your head up and not fall for the con-games and get-rich-quick schemes. If you were not up on your P's & Q's, then you were subject to fall victim to the perpetrator, and he or she would most likely name you "Boo-Boo the Fool." And you would never want to be "Boo-

Boo the Fool," because everyone would try to take a bite out of you, and they would eat you alive. They preyed on the weak and gullible. You really needed to know how to navigate the tough streets of Los Angeles to survive.

As I navigated my way through the courses of my last year of high school, there was one class in particular that sparked my ambition. That was the Reserve Officer Training Corps (ROTC).

My Mom asked, "How are you doing with that military class?"

I replied, "You mean my ROTC class?"

"Yes! So, you want to join the military like your Uncle Conrad?"

"Oh! It's going pretty good. They say that it will help me get into the Army after I'm finished with school. And unlike Uncle Conrad, I'm joining. He was drafted."

"Yeah, your Uncle Conrad served three tours in Vietnam. I would love to see you follow in your father's footsteps."

"That might be good, mom, but things are changing now, so it might be a hard job to do.

"Son, if you put your head to anything, you can do it. Besides, that would make me so proud."

"I would like to make you proud, Momma."

"That's my son! And you should talk with your Uncle Conrad."

"Yeah, Mom. I'll call him up."

My Uncle Conrad is my mother's brother, a Vietnam veteran who served three tours in the Vietnam war to fight for the country. He was a proud, but bitter veteran. He had a deep love for the country, at the same time carrying a strong grudge against the government. I called him up and he gave me an in-depth description of the ROTC class.

My Uncle answered, "Hello!"

"Hey, Uncle Conrad! This is little Robert!"

"Hey, young-blood. How are you doing?"

"Aw, I'm doing fine. I just wanted to call you about a military class."

"What class is it?"

"It's the ROTC class."

"Yeah, young blood, the ROTC is a class that helps prepare young adults to become officers in the U.S. military after high school."

"So, it will definitely help me with my military career path?"

"Yes, the class will teach you character education, student achievement, wellness, leadership, and diversity. Collectively, these lessons will help motivate you to become a good citizen for your country! Young-blood!"

"Okay, cool. Thanks for the information, Uncle Conrad."

"Hey, no problem, young-blood! Good to see you going in this route. They want to feed the young-bloods with basketball and other sports while the white boys are joining the armed forces to enforce the American law and order."

"I understand you, Uncle Conrad. I understand."

"Okay, young-blood one love!"

The class would always have me wondering about my father. Since I never met him; my curiosity of him led me to want to take the same career path that he took and make my mother proud once I left high school.

"Have you thought about how you're going to spend your summer?" my mom asked. You know it's going to be a hot one."

I responded, "I thought 'bout signing up for a summer job, working at the school again like I did last summer."

"Well, that's good, but you know you're going to have to start looking for something more permanent. Your school days are coming to an end."

"I'm still thinking about joining the Army as a recruit for a military police. My ROTC teacher said that he could help me with that career path. And that will satisfy your ideas for me too. What do you think?"

"That's sounds great!"

I actually skipped out on the senior high school activities, like senior prom, due to the fact I was more of an introvert. However, I was more than anti-social; some would call me a Black nerd. So, once graduation was over, I spent the summer in the big city, working as a maintenance worker at the 116th Street School, cleaning up classrooms, scrubbing graffiti and gum off the tables and walls, and stripping the floors. In the middle of summer, I got in touch with my army recruiter to enlist into the U.S. Army. As I went through the recruitment and enlistment process with testing, I tested for the Military Police (MP) for a three-year term, keeping my father in mind as I passed the test and got placed.

"Hip hip hooray! Today is your day, son! I'm so proud of you! Are you all packed for your trip?"

"Thanks, Mom! I'm all packed and a little excited and nervous about the trip. I mean the airplane ride."

"Boy! It isn't anything to it! Just buckle your seatbelt and go to sleep. You'll be there in no time!"

"All right, Mom, if you say so."

My date for entering the U.S. Army was July 5, 1983, a day after celebrating our great country's birthday, and boy, I had never felt prouder. My mother and I were very excited that I was going off to serve my country, and I was ready to defend the Constitution against all enemies— foreign, or domestic—and protect America's freedoms.

My Father

Chapter 2

The Red, White, and Blue

I was assigned to Fort McClellan for basic combat training; it was adjacent to the city of Anniston, Alabama. Fort McClellan trains over 40,000 young recruits in any year. It was a drastic change from Los Angeles and the ROTC back at Locke High School. Fort McClellan had a very diverse and ethnic group of recruits; however, I was there to be one of the best soldiers my country could produce. Combat training was very demanding, but it was well worth it.

I entered into the red, white, and blue phases of boot camp as recruits arrived for general orientation and were given haircuts and issued Army uniforms. The Army made sure every recruit was physically and mentally prepared to start basic combat training. Within 17 weeks I became physically and mentally stronger, and very well trained in tactical weapons and counter terrorism for operational units in hostile and obscure environments. I had field training exercises, confidence obstacle courses, and tactical foot marches. I became a professional rifle marksman after becoming familiar with the use of automatic weapons and hand grenades in weapons training.

I learned to live the Seven Core Army Values, which was the foundation instilled in all soldiers upon entry to the U.S. Army. The Seven Core Army Values make soldiers of our free nation reliable in battle. LDRSHIP is the acronym for these values:

LOYALTY: Bear true faith and allegiance to the U.S. Constitution.

DUTY: Fulfill your obligations.

RESPECT: Treat people as they should be treated.

SELFLESS SERVICE: Put the welfare of the nation, the Army, and your subordinates before your own.

HONOR: Live up to all the Army values.

INTEGRITY: Do what's right, legally, and morally.

PERSONAL COURAGE: Face fear, danger, or adversity, both physical and moral.

Basic combat training pushed my mind and body to new limits; it gave me a deeper respect for myself and those around me. As I transitioned from civilian to soldier, I lost some weight, trimmed down, had my **Jeri curl** cut down to a bald head, and traded my glasses in for contact lenses. I felt like I was a real badass by the time I was finished with basic training.

I was transferred to Fort Jackson, South Carolina, the deep South, as I could recall my mother would call it, when she would lecture me on the reason she and father were chased out of the deep South of Shreveport, Louisiana back when they were young adults. My father had gotten into a fight with a white guy at a local thrift store while he was trying on some clothes before he bought them. It was against the law for any Black person to try on clothes at a store before they bought them.

"Hey, nigger boy! What do you think you're doing?"

"What? I'm trying on this coat to see if I can wear it!"

"You know you niggers not supposed to be putting on no clothes!"

"Mind your business, Sir! I'm trying to see if it fits."

"That is my business, boy! And you can't be trying on no clothes!"

"I know what I'm supposed to be doing!"

"Oh! You're a smart-ass nigger! Well, you take that! Boy!"

"Got damn it! I'm going to kick your ass for that!"

"You just c'mon, nigger, c'mon!"

"You asked for it got-damn it!"

"Oh, shit, nigger! You struck me in the mouth! You motherfucker!"

"Hey, let's get that nigger!"

"Hey Boy! What are you doing striking that white man? We're going to kick your ass, nigger!"

The guy yelled at my father and punched him in the mouth, as my father returned the same punishment to him. That's when all hell broke loose. Every white person in the vicinity joined in. They helped the white guy to beat my father. The white guy was in distress trying to fight my father. Those people beat the holy shit out of my father. They took turns punching, kicking, and spitting on him. Women and men. They ripped off his shirt, and as the mob grew tired of the physical abuse they were giving my father; he managed to surreptitiously escape from their violent attack.

Bam! Bam! Bam!

"Honey! Honey! Open up! Open up!"

"Okay! Dear! Okay! I'm here! What happened, Robert? What happened?"

"I got into a scuffle with a white fella! And what seemed like the whole town began to beat on me Mary! We must get out of here! We got to go Mary! Tonight!"

"Okay Robert! Okay! I'll gather our things!"

Although he managed to make it home in shock and disbelief, battered and bruised, he and my mother gathered up a few of their belongings and slipped away through the night and never looked back.

I always kept her lecture (or should I say, cautionary tale) in the back of my mind as the military community welcomed me when I moved in on base. It seemed like a tight-knit military community ready to welcome me with open arms. It was definitely a change from south-central Los Angeles. However, I had to stay focused on what I was in the U.S. Army for and that was to become a military police officer and to protect my country from all enemies, foreign and domestic. My job consisted of carrying a 9mm Beretta semi-automatic pistol weapon with live ammunition every day, writing tickets for military members, patrolling, and carrying out the law on the military base. The military is essentially a job except that I could go to jail if I was late for reporting to my post. I could be considered absent without leave (AWOL). I got some free time to spend with associates and I would socialize mostly with the Black soldiers. I felt that I would have an easier connection. I also took part in sports or hobbies. I also managed to obtain my driver's license.

I entered a self-promotion program and tried to become a little better than my peers. So, I took college courses, and military correspondence courses to get ahead of some of my peers. I didn't have any friends at the time, as I was really focused on my studies and job details. I was still listening to my rhythm and blues and rap music on my earphones. I had Marvin Gaye and the Sugar Hill Gang in rotation.

I happened to meet Christopher Johnson. He was a fellow Black soldier from Tallahassee, Florida, when I was in the barracks singing "Let's Get It On," out loud with my earphones on.

"Let's Get It On," I sang soulfully.

The soldier said, "Hey man! You're messing up the song!"

"What? You talking to me? What did you say?"

"I said you're messing up Marvin Gaye's song!"

"Hey man! This shit sounds good!"

"Yeah, but you should just let Marvin sing it, because you're not doing a good job at it."

"Oh Yeah? You think you can do better?"

"Nah man, I'm not a singer, and it's obvious you're not either!" (Laughing)

"Aw man, forget you!"

"Hey man, my apology man! What's happening, man, I love Marvin Gaye too. Hey man, my name is Christopher Johnson from Tallahassee. They call me CJ. What's yours?"

"I'm Robert Smith Los Angeles. How long have you been in for?"

"I've been in the Army for two years now. How about you?"

"I've been in for about a year now. Hey man, we should hang out sometime."

"Hey yeah! We can go to town with some of the other fellas."

I would go out occasionally to catch a movie with some of my associates and fellow soldiers. That is when I met Mark Koon. Mark was an MP as well. He was a big white guy with an orange tan, who stood 6'2' tall, 210 pounds, and had a heavy southern drawl along with a peculiar disposition. As a proud native of South Carolina, he wore a tattoo of the confederate flag on his right arm and a tattoo of the American flag on his left arm. He seemed to be a friendly guy.

He reached out to CJ and me. "Hey, fellas! Are you joining the boys in taking in a movie and maybe hit the bar? We'd love to have ya!"

"Yeah! Why not! It's my birthday as well! Hey, by the way what's your name?"

"I'm Mark, Mark Koon from right here in South Carolina; and yours?"

"I'm Robert Smith from California, and this is CJ from Tallahassee."

Although I told him my name was Robert, he would call me Bob or Bobby. I noticed when we would hang around the other soldiers out on a small leave, he would love to go into a sort of comedic personality. I could understand the name Bob. It was short for Robert; some folks would call me Bobby. But I never understood how he came up with the name Dan until Mark and I, along with a group of other soldiers, were out on leave. We were over in the nearest town catching a movie and hitting the bars for my 21st birthday, which is February 12th. I will never forget that birthday. That's when I had my first drink of alcohol in the Salamander Bar and Grill. I was drinking tequila and America's best beer, Budweiser. We were enjoying our drinks. With an all-white American country music band blaring through the loudspeakers, one of the soldiers insisted on going over to the nearest whorehouse. It was called The Purring Kitten Cathouse. It would be a rite of passage to sow my wild oats. I was becoming a 21-year-old real man. I immediately became overwhelmed from the idea of having intercourse for the first time in my life. However, the drinks and the peer pressure had my ambitions and courage at a level so high I knew that I was near "Cloud 9." One of the soldiers shouted out "the ladies in that whorehouse love a man in uniform." Mark strongly disagreed immediately with the whole idea. He was basically telling the Black soldiers there was no way for them to get into the whorehouse. However, I was willing to bet him that we do get in. Mark began to say no, and I began to disagree.

Mark shouted, "Hell no! We all can't get into the whorehouse!"

In my feel-good state, I responded, "The hell we can't! I say let's give it a try!"

"I said, we all cannot get in!"

"I'm willing to bet we all get in!"

"That's not the point! Look here, Bobby. You and CJ are going to have to go across the tracks to the backwoods blues shacks. You fellas can find Black whores there. I need you Black fellas to go in separate directions. When it comes down to having sex with those white whores, we down here in South Carolina don't agree with any of that California shit!"

"Hey, man! I don't know my way around here, and I don't know about the other fella, but I'm staying with the group!"

I had no idea and no knowledge of which direction to go to find the blues shacks Mark was speaking about. I must have had too much to drink. I insisted on going to that one and only whorehouse in that town. As we approached the door, CJ and I were immediately dismissed and refused entry without discussion. The white soldiers entered the whorehouse without hesitation. CJ turned around and caught a cab back to base.

I stood there and started to yell out Mark's name and began to curse him out over the loud country music.

Mark stopped and turned around and came outside to where I was standing. He approached me and began to plead and beg by telling me that this is against his belief.

"Hey man! I told you! You need to go find some Black pussy! We don't believe in that Black and white sex shit down here!"

"Man, I thought you were cool! You giving me some bullshit about your bullshit belief!"

"Okay, man! However, I'm going to need an extra twenty dollars. One is to get you in the door. The other one is for my pocket."

"Okay man, no problem! Hey man! I'm sorry about your beliefs!"

He gave the extra twenty dollars to the old white guy who was working the door.

"He's with me."

I smiled at the old white guy and walked by. Mark and I entered the whorehouse. I followed behind Mark as he guided me through the place. The Purring Kitten was filled with white whores cladded in negligees. Loud country music was blaring through the speakers. There was a variety of small rooms with large beds inside. We met up with the other soldiers. The group started to question Mark on his whereabouts since entering the whorehouse.

"Hey! What took you so long? We didn't know where you went."

Mark began to explain to the group over the loud music, "I had to help get that Dumb Ass Nigger in!" just as one of the other white soldiers yelled out "Dan!"

So, that's when I understood where the name Dan came from. Some of the white soldiers were calling the Black soldiers Dan for the acronym of Dumb Ass Nigger. When I overheard the conversation, I made up in my mind to make my way to the nearest restroom, where I had an intervention with myself. As I exited the restroom, I had made up my mind to have sex with one of those white whores in that whorehouse, knowing that my fellow white soldiers would be a little irritated with me due to their beliefs.

I chose Tabitha. She was a pretty little young white girl about 22 years old, weighing around 110 pounds. She had a bronze tan and was wearing a nice purple negligee and a blonde shoulder length wig.

"Hello, are you available tonight?"

"Why of course fella!"

"Okay, I have the money."

"No, no you don't need money anymore; you can have any one of these ladies here once you paid to get in here."

"Wow! Umm! Where do we go from here?"

"Follow me."

She led me to a small room with a blue light on inside.

"Take off your hat and shoes."

"Okay, that's it?"

"No, I'll help you undress."

"All right great!"

"Lie down on the bed and take off your shirt."

"What about my pants?"

"I'll help you with those."

I followed Tabitha's every instruction; I enjoyed Tabitha giving me the directions.

By the time I had my shirt off, Tabitha was working on my zipper. Midway down she reached her hand inside my pants. She stared me right in my eyes and began to ask me questions while stroking and pulling on my penis.

"Do you like this?"

"Yes! Don't stop!"

"Something tells me that you don't do this often."

"I never had someone else to do this for me."

"Well tonight you have me to take care of everything. Lay back."

Once I had a good erection, Tabitha helped herself by slipping a condom onto my penis. She climbed on the bed. She sat right on my penis, I held on to her waist with both hands. She rolled and rocked her body back and forth. She kind of coached me through the process. I happened to remove the wig from her head. To my surprise she was a brunette underneath the wig. I felt that brunette girls looked better than blonde women. So, I asked her to keep the wig off to better satisfy my appetite for the night.

"Oh, I'm sorry!" I said.

"Aw, it's no problem! I wear it because a lot of the soldiers prefer a blonde."

"I like your dark hair. Can you leave it off?"

"Yes, no problem. Whatever you want."

"Yeah, I like that."

Tabitha left the wig on the floor along with everything else that she wore in the room. She took the lead and I followed. She confided in me that I was her first African American soldier in her career of whoring. I, in return, confided in her that she was my first experience with sex outside of using my imagination.

Once my introduction into real sex was complete, Tabitha and I spent an extra hour indulging in heavy drinking, and just talking about racial differences in America. Tabitha turned out to be a really nice young lady of the night. I could imagine her as a professional social therapist of some kind as we kissed and said our goodbyes.

I was drunk and stumbling around as I managed to pay up for my extra liquor bill and for the extra time that I spent with Tabitha, I walked outside and hailed down a cab to get me back to the base. I made it back to the barracks, and once I was in my bed I immediately passed out, only to be briefly awakened and knocked out again from the blows of stones embedded in socks used as weapons to beat me until I was in critical condition. Some of my so-called fellow soldiers called it a sock party.

"Get his ass. We are going to teach his ass about our beliefs. Hold him down! We're not playing with your Black ass nigger!"

"I wish we had a rope to hang his ass! Get his ass! Hold him down!"

"Beat his ass! Got damn it!"

"Yeah! We're giving his ass a sock party!"

"You like fucking white women? Yeah, take this!"

Usually they would catch a person asleep in bed and somehow restrain him, and as he's held down, strike repeatedly, using a sock or a bath towel containing stones or bars of soap. Once I came to, I was lying in the infirmary with multiple bruises all over my body, along with two cracked ribs. I stayed there for two and a half weeks. I was told by one of the white medics that I was beaten by a group of soldiers. They didn't like the idea of me having sex and spending my birthday with a white girl, according to them.

"Hey Sir," the medic said. "I'm sorry for what happened to you, but those fellas didn't like you having sex with that white gal."

"Hey man! I was just out trying to have some fun with my fellow soldiers."

"Not with those guys man! They are a bunch of racist fellas."

"They seemed cool!"

"You were supposed to go across the tracks to the ghetto and find a Black whore."

"Those particular soldiers are not real "American" soldiers! They are race-soldiers!"

"I didn't know that I was walking such a fine line. I just insisted on going into that whorehouse with those white whores, that's all. I didn't realize I was in uncharted waters!"

"I advise you man! Mark Koon is leading the pack! They are a group of white racists! They are hypersensitive about inferiority toward the dominant gene."

"So, you're telling me that they joined the United States Army to impose their views and beliefs across the United States?"

"Yes! And around the world, knowing that the United States is a superpower around the world."

"Wow, okay they hate Black people!"

"Yes, you have to understand that! You be careful!"

"Thanks man!"

As soon as I was released from the infirmary, I went to report the group of soldiers. However, I could not identify any of them. I was so drunk and passed out when they attacked me. I was also told that the word around the base was that I got attacked on my way back from the whorehouse, which I knew wasn't true. I knew from that day on I could never trust too many of my fellow soldiers. Some of them could not look me in the eyes. But I had a job to do and my country to protect, although I did not see any wartime or combat during my time in the Army.

Chapter 3

Law and Order

I continued to hold a grudge; I had to move on with my duties in the military. I still had an appetite for law and justice running through my veins, due to my conflict with Mark and the race-soldiers. I was relocated to other military bases throughout the continental U.S. Finally, I was moving towards ending my military career path. I was a grown man fully equipped with an educational background and tactical military training, and really did not know what to do with it. I was destitute. My mother took a personal interest in making sure that I made a smooth transition back into civilian life. Once I was discharged, my mother asked me to join the Los Angeles Police Department (LAPD).

From the time I left high school until now, the man in office had been President Ronald Reagan, whose views I did not particularly care for. When Ronald Reagan was the governor of California, he, along with then President Richard Nixon, both proclaimed to be the law-and-order governor and president. They were overheard on a phone call, laughing and talking about Black people, calling them "monkeys from African countries." The term "law-and-order" has always been synonymous with a war on the

Black communities in America. And usually, the sentiments of the president trickles down to city law enforcement.

"I'm so glad to have you back home, son."

"Thanks, Mom, but you know a man stands before you now. I'm glad to be back home! Checking out the city, Mom, things have changed a lot!"

"Yeah, some things got a little better. Then too, some things have gotten worse!"

"That's the big city for you."

"Now that your military career is over, we can sure use your help in the big city!"

"Yeah? Doing what?"

"They can use your help in the LAPD."

"Okay, Mom, let me think about it. I just got home."

"There is nothing to think about. I thought that was what you wanted to do? Just like your daddy?"

"Yeah, but things have really changed since then, I'll give it some thought."

"Okay! Don't wait too long!"

My mother had always said how she would love to see me help combat the growing crime that was surrounding my old neighborhood and community. She also thought that it was an admirable profession.

By this time, the war on the Black community in Los Angeles was in full effect. President Reagan, along with the Congress of the United States of America declared a national crusade against drugs. It was later discovered that Reagan was playing both sides of the chessboard. Through what Congress and President Reagan called the Iran-Contra Affair, they escalated the crusade against drugs on Black people by supplying the communities with drugs. This was an actual cat and mouse game to destroy the communities. The scandal hit the Black section hard in 1987, just about the time when my mother wanted me to join the Los Angeles Police Department. The government used the money from drug sales in the Black communities to purchase guns/weapons and gave them to the anti-communist Contras in Nicaragua. The money was not in the government's budget, so that's the path they took. The United States needed to have control of that part of the world before the communist Russians took control. It was a real live chess game with the Nicaraguans and Black American communities being the pawns.

I thought deeply about that occupation my mother said she would love to see me have, knowing that she always wanted to see me do better. I was confronted with a pivotal decision. And instead, I thought about my gangbanging cousins and the mean gangster guys I grew up with up and down Avalon Boulevard. I had my father on my mind when my mother looked me in my eyes and damn near begged me to help her and the Los Angeles South Central community. I thought to myself that was the reason

I joined the army and became an MP, following in my father's footsteps. Then I thought about the way my father died. The streets of Los Angeles can be very tricky in the beautiful sunshine and lovely weather while the citizens are living their daily lives.

I knew that being a cop on the streets of Los Angeles would be a much bigger task than working my post in the military. I knew that this wasn't just a Los Angeles problem; the whole country could use an overhaul. I thought about domestic violence, drug dealers, traffic stops, and homicides. My mother told me that working and dealing with those issues were some of the things that made my father the great man he was. He loved to serve the city and community.

"You know your father went out there! And he fought crime in those streets like nobody's business! That was one of the things that made him a great man!"

"Yeah, Mama, I know. You tell me that all the time."

"Your daddy was such a great man."

So, as I applied to LAPD, I felt a sense of pride creep into my veins. With the military police experience and high-tech weaponry training, I was immediately hired. It was a smooth transition from the Army right into the LAPD When I was first hired, I met all the minimum requirements and passed the law enforcement entrance exam, then graduated from the police academy. After all the blood, sweat, and tears, earning my police badge felt dignifying. I was sworn to defend and protect people. I'd arrest and detain individuals who are accused of breaking the law. I'd ensure drivers are following traffic laws, respond to emergencies, and patrol areas where crimes may occur. I'd often document any action I took in a detailed report. Once I was out in the field the excuses ended and the training lessons began. I became a professional in the community's eye.

I lived with my mother as she moved from the old neighborhood into the city of Gardena, California, just under 12 miles from where I grew up. In a small, one-room apartment, I slept on her sofa bed for about a year, until, with my Veterans Affairs loan, I managed to buy a small home in the city of Carson, California, four miles away from her. It was single-family stucco English-styled home with a living room, small kitchen, two-small bedrooms, and a basement. It had a detached garage and there was a tiny back yard.

My mother stayed active with the neighborhood watch programs around Los Angeles. She kept in contact with her friends and they would call her on the phone, giving her the 411 about what was going on and keeping her in the loop.

"Girl, you know we have to continue to stay vigilant."

"Yeah, honey, I know!"

"These streets are changing for the worst!"

"Yeah, and the police aren't any better."

The first year on the force, I was really trying to get adjusted to the transitional period and finding my footing. In my second year I was still trying to find my groove with dealing with the community. It was almost like people management. Whatever the case may be, it was important to display a positive attitude. I've always showcased my enthusiasm, thinking it will likely draw in my co-workers and partner, making interactions a bit smoother with the community. I would hang out at the bars where only cops hung out. We would exchange street stories on the daily.

However, I was struggling and barely getting by as a rookie cop living on a rookie cop's salary. I was trying to make my monthly mortgage and supply myself with the living necessities. I didn't own a car to get around in. I used the department's car to get around.

On this one day at the end of my shift, I happened to see and ask Theodore Campbell, who was Chief of Police at the time, how I could increase my monthly pay.

"Hey, Chief Campbell, can I have a word with you?"

"What is it, Smith?"

"Sir, I was wondering how to get a promotion or a raise? I need a little bit more money."

"Well, I'll tell you what I tell all of my officers. You have to really patrol those people out there! You have to really give me something in exchange for a good salary."

"I thought that I was doing my job well. I guess I wasn't?"

"That's not what I really need. I want you to go out there and mix it up a bit, engage the community more, show them who is boss! Don't just patrol! You have to dominate them with law and order!"

"Okay, I see. Sure thing, sure thing, sir! I get your point!"

Law enforcement is much like the military when it comes down to following orders. It was important to follow orders; therefore, respect and obedience is of utmost importance. He instructed me to really come down hard on the citizens. Chief Campbell wanted to create a structure in the department that would disenfranchise the Black community. With writing more tickets and citations, and making more arrests each month, I could give myself a pay raise and maximize my income. Subsequently, I purchased a used black and red 1982 Ford Mustang. I was incentivized and law and conflict had justified me.

I really had to take advantage of some of the citizens when they didn't know or understand the law. I was taught to move in a provoking manner to cause a conflict in order to get what I wanted; therefore, I'd be justified by law. I was taught to express to the citizens that ignorance of the law is no excuse. The more tickets and citations I wrote or the more arrests I made, the greater chance I had in enhancing my salary each month. If there was a citizen caught with a firearm, it was an extra bonus for my paycheck. Disarming Black America was top priority in law enforcement. It wasn't really about gang violence, but the interest of the safety of the surrounding white communities like Torrance, California. If I caught a citizen drunk in public, that would help me as well. A broken taillight or domestic disturbance would all help my paycheck. I needed to make my monthly quota so bad; I began to not allow any passes. I would not issue any warnings to the citizens.

"Do you know why I'm writing you this ticket?"

"No, Sir. I was just walking to the store."

"Yeah, and I saw you jaywalk across the street too."

"Yeah, but you didn't cross in the crosswalk. So, I need you to sign this ticket and you'll be free to go."

"Wow, a ticket for just crossing the street? This shit don't make no sense."

"Hey! Do you want to go to jail? Now you're free to go!"

My partner, Officer Seth O'Malley (white guy), and I would focus more on pretextual routine stops, giving us the green light to do a more thorough search, which would give us a better chance at making an arrest simply on a search of a vehicle. We were sure to find something! They would occur when we wished to investigate a motorist on other suspicions, generally related to drug and firearms possession. We used a minor traffic infraction as a pretext to stop the driver. If there were no criminal behavior or criminal offense, we would search for numerous petty violations. If not, we'd manufacture one. We would be selective about who we pulled over and investigated. It would typically go like this.

"Waaaaahhhhhh." (Siren)

"Cut off the radio and the car; let me see your license and registration. I pulled you over because you were speeding. Do you know how fast you are going?"

"I'm sorry officer, I don't know. I must have gotten lost into the music "

"Yeah, well sit there with your hands where I can see them. "

"Sir, l believe I wasn't doing no more than 5 miles over the speed limit."

"Oh, yeah? You want to be a jackass; I deal with jackasses every day. Get out! I need to search you and the vehicle for drugs and weapons "

"Man! You have no right to search my car."

"I'm the fucking police; I have the right to do whatever I want to do. Turn around and shut your mouth. Search the vehicle, O'Malley."

"Officer, I don't have any drugs or weapons in my car. Don't you guys have anything better to do?"

"Yeah, we have something better to do. I'm going to give you a ticket for the dark tint on your car windows and a broken taillight"

"My taillight isn't broken!"

The officer breaks the taillight with his baton "It's broken now! So, sign this ticket!"

"This is bullshit!"

"You have a good day now!"

As a cop, I became a pariah on the streets of my own city. Due to the teaching of my colleagues and superiors, I was working to clean up the Los Angeles streets the hard way.

It was really taking a toll on my conscience. I was sending a lot of my people straight to jail for little or nothing. However, I felt absolutely pleased when I would arrest the suspected big dope dealers and suspected killers. That would sort of clear up some of the guilt that was running through my mind from time to time. I knew I wasn't working the streets as an upright cop like I pictured my father was before he was killed.

"Hold it! I saw you hand that kid that crack rock! I'm taking you down for a long time, pal!"

"Hey, man! That was just a few pebbles. That's all!"

"Yeah, man! And you are getting kids hooked on that shit!"

"Aww man! You got to be kidding me!"

"No, I'm not! Get your dope pushing ass in the car!"

I never participated in any of the big money shakedowns from the big-time dope dealers who were going down. I would never go that far, although the extra money was needed. I felt so good running my own city streets as a cop. I knew the city streets and alleyways from the seedy areas of town to the upscale parts of town. I knew that the upscale part of town was where the real good dope and so-called white-collar crimes were. They were nestled away from the national news and television stations.

We would consider Vermont Avenue between Florence Avenue and Manchester Boulevard, to be our playground. We had pimps and whores to bust on prostitution and petty drug dealing. That's when we knew that we could have the whores for free. We would pretend to attempt to arrest them for prostitution after all the pleasure was over.

"You know we should take you girls in! But, since you've treated me and my partner so nicely, we're going let you girls off with a warning."

"Thank you! Mister Officers! We'll be good girls!"

"You don't talk about this to no one! Or we will have you arrested!"

"Sure, Mister Officer!"

"Okay! Y'all free to go!"

"Man! O'Malley we really need to bring some tickets and citations in, one-way or another! And have some fun doing it! Man! You hear me?"

"Hey. man! I don't give a damn what I have to do to make the quota! These are your people!"

The whole city police force led by Chief Campbell, from the highest to the very lowest ranking officer was contaminated by corruption in one way or another. Cops robbed citizens and planted drugs on them as well, under protection of their badges. The scandals only reinforced the community's deep distrust of the police department at a time when widespread policing was out of control. We claimed massive amounts of overtime for hours we did not work. A series of crimes that were being committed by the cops on the streets of Los Angeles were due to the very high cost of living and greed. The cops were living on a very low salary. The same city that we were paid to serve and protect, the streets of Los Angeles, were like the Wild West. The mayor, Tom Bradley himself, could not clean up the mess. The protagonist relationship that the news media had with law enforcement to support policies that criminalized Black people had begun to take place.

My mother and her neighborhood watch program got involved. They began to galvanize throughout the city and take action with an urgency to save the community. She knew a lot of the wrongdoing that was going on was not just perpetrated by the citizens; it was the city police officers who were allowed to roam the streets.

It was not good when her very own son was among those bad apples of cops. Although it wasn't just citizens committing all the crimes, my mother's organization held sworn officers to a high standard. Her organization was trying to eradicate a few bad apples as cops from the community. Some were trying to make it and get by through dirty deeds by any means.

America's apple pie was baked with some bad apples. Many cops were resigning and just walking off the job due to substandard wages caused by work overload or being fired due to crooked dealings and being caught with their hands in the cookie jar due to illicit behavior.

I had an inner conflict I had to wrestle with. I would often think to myself about the choices I had to make: either clean up my act as a sworn officer and do right by my oath and community or continue to be a part of a cesspool of a police department and one day maybe ruin my legacy along with my father's.

"Hey O'Malley, I've been thinking about the way we've been treating the community. I don't believe I personally can continue doing this shit!

"Hey, man! We are just making our jobs fun while we are doing it! You know?"

"Man, this is not sitting well with me! I know a lot of these people. It's just not cool, man!"

"Yeah, man! I see your point. After all, these are your people! Cool!"

"We really have to stop this shit! It's not what we signed up for!

"Okay, Bobby; I got your back!"

On the very day I was having a meeting of the minds, knowing my course of actions would someday lead me to inevitable unintended consequences, my mother gave me a call to come over to her house. She somehow knew that I was in a bad situation, dealing with misconduct. As I entered my mother's home, a group of her friends and members of the neighborhood watch program unpleasantly surprised me. Triggering me into an excessive sweating episode, feeling that someone exposed my hidden secrets. It turned out be an intervention to get me to straighten up my act and get on the right path.

"Robert, I invited you here to discuss some things I've been told. Now, I'm not accusing you of anything, son, but I need the truth from you. Son, I've been hearing that you've been abusing your power as a cop. Is that true son? And if this is the truth, son, that's not the vision I had in mind for you."

"Momma, to be honest with you, I've been doing some wrong things out there as a cop. But I am straightening up my act — my partner and I."

"Son, that's not how I raised you! All I'm saying to you is use your humanity and uphold your oath! I want better from you, son! You understand me?"

"Yes, I do understand your words and I'm truly remorseful for my behavior. I will stand by my oath"

As an officer and as my mother's son, it was embarrassing to her in front of her organization, knowing how she forced me to do better than what I was doing. I was no longer a young boy doing wrong. I was a man. That's the way she saw me when she cursed me out, for behaving like an asshole cop. My mother and her organization convinced me to get my shit together and do right by my community. I had to recognize the errors of my ways. I realized that my mother had heard about some of my wayward behavior while out patrolling the street. A neighborhood watch member reported me to my mother, of all people.

I agreed to clean up my act and try to persuade many of my fellow officers to do the same; I also took on a second job doing security work part-time for some of the well-known Hollywood celebrities to add to my income. Throughout the years, Hollywood had cleaned up their seedy areas, unlike in the old days when my father had patrolled the city. Hollywood and the citizens were a little more upscale by now. Therefore, other surrounding cities near Hollywood were treated on the same level as Chinatown, Koreatown, Little Italy, and even East Los Angeles. Not one of those cities was treated with the heavy hand of law enforcement like that of south-central. The uptick in unfair policing was a widespread phenomenon in the African American community. And south-central Los Angeles was made out to be the worst part of the city. I began to focus on ensuring that African Americans fully participate in the benefits of this society and their lives flourish, just like the neighboring communities that surround the south-central. We needed a fair balance in enforcing the law.

Chapter 4

Amy Freeman and the Race-Soldiers

As the relationship between law enforcement and the community of Los Angeles was on a down swing and had begun to fray, I had fallen for an attractive southern belle by the name of Amy Freeman. She was a pretty 27-year-old white brunette, who was raised in the South and very polite, as she would respond with yes ma'am, no ma'am.

She was one of my colleagues. As we spent a tremendous amount of time at work together, we would share vulnerable conversations; there was no doubt that a romantic relationship was brewing. Common sense did not tell me to avoid an office romance, and I knew it might reflect poorly on both of us and become awkward if things didn't work out. It was a good thing that the department did not have any explicit policies against dating co-workers.

"Hello, I'm Officer Robert Smith; I've been on the force for about four years now and if you need any help with anything, just let me know."

"Well, I will do just that! "

"I'm serious. Call on me when you need anything! I'm your guy. (Smiles)"

"I think you are! But we will see."

"Here's my number. I'm just a call away."

"Sure thing!" Maybe you can show me around the city."

"Hey, no problem! This is my city, born and raised"

"That's great to hear, I feel secure already"

"I'm telling you I'm your guy"

"Okay! Okay! We'll talk about it."

She kind of reminded me of Tabitha from my military days. She was a new recruit on the LAPD and had been transferred from Birmingham, Alabama. She had a southern accent. She was also a very smart lady. She held a law degree in civil rights. I've gone through some very financially humbling times, but it never affected my desire to date. I could afford a fancy dinner for two, but I didn't want her to break the bank. However, dating reinforced the importance of our relationship. She liked to go out dancing, but I was a flatfooted wallflower. We would be so tired from spending the night on the town that Amy would often spend the night and head off to work from my home.

Things got cozy. I presented Amy with a key to my house, which allowed her to come and go as she pleased. Soon Amy and I grew so close she moved in with me. We shared the utility bills to make ends meet and still remained lovers. She would cook southern soul food dishes like smothered pork chops, collard greens, and peach cobbler. She would have the kitchen smelling just like my mother used to have it when I was younger.

"Aww! That smell takes me back to my childhood; it smells so good," I exclaimed to Amy.

"Yeah, baby you better come in here and get some of my smothered pork chops and collard greens," she replied.

"You don't have to say anymore. I want my share right now."

"Here you go! And let's say our blessings."

"Yes, Lord thank you for this meal that sits before me. Amen"

"I hope you enjoy the meal "

"Oh, yeah! I'm sure I will."

"Okay!" Didn't fill up with too much; you have to stay fit for work"

"I'm not worried about that! I'll work it off."

"Okay, I'll love you anyway."

"Yeah, I love you too babe."

Although we did not work together as we patrolled the city, our relationship strengthened. I had to assure Amy's parents that she was in good hands with living and dating me, so we arranged a meet and greet by flying Amy's parents, Mr. and Mrs. Freeman, into Los Angeles, where we set them up in a hotel room near the Los Angeles airport.

"Hello Mr. Freeman. I'm Robert Smith. Welcome to Los Angeles. Hope your flight was pleasant."

"Nice to meet you. The flight was pleasant and everything was comfortable. This is my wife, Susanne."

"Can I help you with anything?" Robert asked.

Mrs. Freeman spoke with a pleasant voice.

"Nice to meet you. I'm okay; I just need to rest my feet."

"Okay, come on in the room and take it easy. I've got your luggage."

"Thanks sugar."

Amy's parents were a couple of nice and intelligent people. Amy's mother was a very small middle-aged woman with dark brown hair. By contrast, Amy's father, Mr. Freeman, was a very tall, stern, red-haired gentlemen with the looks of a retired boxer or wrestler but with compassion all at the same time as he expressed his love and concern for Amy living in the big city of Los Angeles as a part of the LAPD. He never mentioned the interracial relationship his daughter was involved in. He did not hesitate to mention his elite organization, which handles personal situations outside of the law on personal levels. Some would call a syndicate.

"You know; if you guys have any misunderstanding here in Los Angeles that you can't handle, please give me a call. I'm sure I can get it straightened out through my organization," said Mr. Freeman.

"Yes sir! I'll keep you in mind," was my reply.

I guess that was to assure me that, although I was with the LAPD, I could still be in jeopardy if I were ever to cross his daughter by any means. I took it as a kind-hearted threat. Mr. and Ms. Freeman were overall nothing less than genuine with the utmost kindness as they departed and gave us God's blessings.

Amy and I continued to work together on the same page as cops who assured the community of their civil rights. We had to sometimes detain them as suspects or future prisoners. We bonded over intense and controversial arrests, requiring late nights at work and at home, sharing our frustration. We were trying to clean up the community. Even while we were on a movie date we would still carry our weapons as officers. If some type of crime occurred, we would be ready to enforce the law, hopefully without conflict.

"You know, we, as cops, have to be extra careful."

"In what way are you speaking of Amy?"

"While on the job, we have to protect ourselves from our own co-workers."

"Yeah, some of the guys are a little offbeat with a badge."

"Some of them are just weird!"

"Yeah, Chief Campbell wants the whole department to dominate our community."

"I take his views to be a little extreme."

The police department was in great turmoil. We were in desperate need of new and fresh officers as the community began to suffer without real law and order. Some of the petty conflicts grew into much larger situations, and many nuances of injustice had removed basic human rights. The community and local politicians began to come down hard on Chief Campbell. At the time, Chief Campbell was serving his second term in office. His first term had been under scrutiny by the community for officers' use of the choke hold and killing many of the citizens, and being heavy handed while using the nightstick, due to the claim of the consistency of resisting in the progress of an arrest

One of our officers shouted, "Roll call."

Chief Campbell took the floor.

"Listen up officers, there are some of you who are not pulling your weight, and we have the media on our asses, saying that we are losing the war on drugs and crime! My name is on the line; my reelection is on the line! I really need you officers to get out there and bring me what I want! I got an idea to bring in some real good fresh meat to handle the job I need done! Do you understand what I'm saying?"

We all shouted.

"Yes sir!"

"Therefore, you are dismissed."

As new and fresh officers began to apply and get hired, a positive vibe and feel would travel throughout the department. I believe some of the citizens in the community felt a positive vibration on the streets once again as the Black community did many years ago. Cops and the citizens of the community were speaking and communicating with one another without any tension or menacing. Until this one particular day when I recognized this all too familiar face amongst a group of all new white recruits that spoke with a heavy southern drawl.

"Welcome to Los Angeles, fellas! You boys just follow me! We are going to clean up this city! I heard that the natives are a little restless."

"We are on your heels! You just lead the way!"

"You fellas are going to have some fun! We are going to dominate this city!"

"If you say so, we are here to take care of business. The American way, southern style!

It just so happened to be Mark Koon, from my military days, with a group of new and old faces of cops, ready to get to work as officers on the streets of Los Angeles with the police department. I felt my face forming a frown that was beyond my control to disguise. I immediately had flashbacks of that violent conflict of the military days. Mark Koon was leading the pack with his grand bravado, along with some of the same race-soldiers. We both had grown throughout the years and I couldn't help but notice that he had packed on about 50 extra pounds. He extended his hand to shake mine and I could not help but make it brief. And his moist hands made it extra uncomfortable. I really didn't know what to expect from Mark.

"Hey Bobby! Long time no see!"

"What's up, Mark? What brings you to Los Angeles? I thought you were a southern fella."

"Crime calls! I heard you folks need our help with the natives! (Smiles)"

"Oh yeah? You guys help?"

"Yes! According to Chief Campbell!"

"Chief Campbell? I see!"

"Yeah, things have to be handled in this city, the media and Chief Campbell tell us that you're losing the battle."

"I believe we are doing just fine here in Los Angeles."

"Yeah, but we are here now."

We approached each other with pleasant greetings and as we spoke, but I could see that Mark still had the mentality of a ringleader with a very high voltage personality as the race-soldiers looked on with poker faces along with a glimpse of envy. I didn't know if I should raise the alarm to avoid a personal conflict or stay quiet and hope for the best. Whichever path I took I knew there'd be consequences.

In the coming days on Los Angeles city streets things seemed to work in Chief Campbell's favor. The streets were at the mercy of Mark and the race-soldiers.

Mark, patrolling alone, didn't hesitate to lead by example with just three days on the job. He answered a domestic violence call at 232 W. Gramercy Place. As he was approaching the address, Jonathan Jones was sitting on the curb at the corner of Wo. 23rd Street and Gramercy.

When Mark shut off the engine as he parked his squad car, Jonathan stood up and attempted to approach Mark. Mark immediately drew his weapon with one hand and grabbed Jonathan by his neck with the other. He slammed him to the ground face down and placed his knee in his back, with his gun to Jonathan's head. Jonathan tried to explain the domestic situation. Mark was substantially larger in height and weight and had many more choices of action. He felt he had to draw his pistol and wanted to provoke fear into Jonathan.

He pointed his pistol and squeezed the trigger, firing a bullet into Jonathan's head, killing Jonathan as he lay on his stomach with his arms and legs extended out in every direction. His head sat in a puddle of his blood.

The loud gunshot demanded the attention of Jonathan's girlfriend, Sherry Kemp, and many of the neighbors nearby. Sherry ran out of the house and dropped down on her knees to Jonathan's dying side, yelling and screaming for help.

"Hey, back the fuck up boy! Show me your hands!

"Hey man! Okay! Okay! I'm just trying to explain to you what happen man!"

"Get your ass down on the ground boy! You have any weapons or drugs? Why did you walk up on me?"

"Man! I'm trying to tell you my girl threw me out and she won't let me get my clothes."

"Listen I don't give a shit about that, boy! I don't want you approaching me. Do you understand me, boy?"

"Yeah man, I didn't mean any harm."

"Listen next time you see me, you better not walk up on me again boy. You hear me boy! Do you understand me boy!"

"Hey man what I do to deserve this shit?"

"You see this fucking pistol, boy? I'll blow your fucking head off, boy!"

"Yeah man, yeah man, please don't shoot!"

Boom!

"Got damn it, you see what you made me do?"

Radio to headquarters! Headquarters! Come in headquarters!

"This is headquarters; what are you reporting?"

"Headquarters, this is Officer Koon. I'm at 232 W. Gramercy Place. I have shots fired! An officer involved

shooting, fearing for my life! I repeat! I was fearing for my life!"

"We are sending units. I repeat, we're sending units!"

"Oh my God! Why did you shoot him? Help! Help! Someone call 911. Oh my God! Help! Call 911!"

Mark replaced his service weapon in the holster and reached for his walkie-talkie radio. In a frantic tone he reported the shooting to headquarters, saying fearing for his life is what led him to squeezing the trigger.

The result of this was that Mark was justified in the eyes of the current District Attorney (DA), according to his report. The clueless DA believed Mark was actually "afraid for his life." The only person who had a right to be afraid of death was Jonathan Jones on the sidewalk of 232 W Gramercy place.

The law was heavily weighted in favor of officers if they reasonably perceived a threat to themselves or others when they opened fire — even if that belief was mistaken. The DA did not bring charges against Mark for an on-duty shooting.

Some of the citizens were concerned by the DA's reasoning, fearing it might signal to officers that when there is a tussle in close quarters, they could be able to justify opening fire by later claiming the suspect was trying to disarm them.

After Mark was cleared of the shooting death of Jonathan Jones, he patrolled the streets like a notorious crime boss (like Mr. Untouchable). He was surly, dominating the streets of south-central just the way Chief Campbell structured the department.

The race-soldiers were planning to just formulate or allege a belief that the citizens were going for their guns, and they would have a blanket justification for shooting the individual.

In the early morning on patrol, race-soldiers Earl Whitlock and Seth Mahoney stopped at Winchell's Donuts at Manchester and San Pedro. Upon entering the donut shop, Whitlock spotted Samuel Lane through the window, going for a morning jog, wearing earphones while listening to music on his Walkman radio. Whitlock summoned Mahoney to take a look, pointing in Lane's direction.

They agreed to stop Lane and question him. They took off on foot trailing Lane. Lane turned off Manchester on to San Pedro, still enjoying his jog, listening to the music. The race-soldiers yelled out to Lane to stop. Not knowing he was being followed, he continued to jog. Lane didn't hear the demand to stop. Mahoney and Whitlock began gaining speed and pumped with a growing excitement. Mahoney caught up with Lane, tackling him to the ground, destroying his Walkman radio. Lane never knew what hit him. He began to defend himself, believing that he was being attacked. He tussled with Mahoney briefly. Just then, Whitlock piled on, somehow causing Mahoney's revolver to go off, shooting and wounding Mahoney in the elbow.

"Hey Whitlock, what kind of donut do you want? Glazed or Buttermilk?"

"Hey Mahoney! Looka there! I wonder what that boy thinks he's doing"

"I see, he probably just stole something. You know how they are, they steal better in the early morning"

"Yeah, let's check him out, and see what's his excuse for running around here so early this morning"

"Yeah, let's see what he stole today."

"Yeah, let's check him out. We'll come back for the donuts."

"Hey nigger, Hey boy! Slow down and stop! Stop got damn it!

"Go for him, Mahoney! I can't run that fast, got damn fast running niggers!"

"I'm on him! Come here nigger! I got him, Whitlock!"

"Man, what the fuck are you doing? Who the fuck are you? Why did you jump on me motherfucker!"

"Give me a hand, Whitlock. Shut the fuck up! What are you running from? What did you steal?"

"Hold him down, Mahoney! We got him now!"

Boom!

"Shit! I'm hit, Whitlock got damn it! I think you shot me, Whitlock."

"Aww shit I think my weapon fired! Fuck! Were you're hit?"

"Hey Man! I didn't know you guys were cops! My hands are up. Don't shoot. I didn't do anything wrong. I was just jogging and listening to my music."

"I'm hit in the elbow, Whitlock!" I'm hit in the elbow!"

"Boy, you just shot my partner! You going to have to pay."

"Hey man! I didn't shoot anybody! I don't have a gun!"

"Yeah, you did boy, and you are going to pay!"

Samuel Lane, a Vietnam War veteran, once he recognized their uniforms, had attempted to surrender to them by raising his hands over his head. Whitlock responded by shooting him from the rear. A bullet pierced his heart, killing him.

The race-soldiers called the shooting in and wrote it up as an attempt to flee the scene, an assault with a deadly weapon on a police officer and prowling the city in search of women to harass and conduct lewd acts on.

Mahoney and Whitlock both were cleared of any wrongdoing in the process of an arrest.

Amidst the grief, disbelief, and justified outrage at the killing of Black folks, many folks wanted to make sense of what appeared to be senseless police mayhem and violence.

As days and months went on, the police brutality began to escalate. The community's complaints fell on the deaf ears of the DA, giving Chief Campbell a pass, and trusting that he had things under his control.

Race-soldiers Edward Shaw and Peter LaBlock, armed with a no-knock warrant before dawn/early morning, executed a raid on the home of Kenny Brown and his wife Sharon Brown, 5233 S Normandie Avenue, on suspicion of drug activity.

"Park the car here, Shaw, and we'll walk up the street to the house, so they won't see us coming"

"Yeah, good idea. I'll get the battle ram from the trunk to knock down the door."

"No! I have a better idea! We should use the flash-grenade. Then they will never know what hit them."

"You damn right! We're going to hit them hard before they can open their eyes!"

"I'll throw the flash-grenade and if they try to run, we're going to blow their fucking heads off!"

"You got damn right! We got them now!"

"Okay, we're here, now throw the fucker through the window, LaBlock!"

Crash boom!

"That's it! Damn it! This fucker's on fire!"

Kenny Brown ran out of the house yelling, "Help! Help! Good Lord help us! Help! My house is on fire! God almighty! Help!"

Race-soldier Edward Shaw yelled, "Hold it! Hold it right there!"

"Oh, thank God you're here! My house is on fire! And my wife's still in there! Please good God! She might be trapped inside! She was just behind me; she must have fallen. Now she's trapped! Call the fire department! Please help my wife! My house is on fire!"

Race-soldier Edward Shaw stated, "We see that and you're under arrest! For drug dealing, Mr. Cadillac Man! You're going down for drug dealing!"

"What! What are you talking about, son? I'm a man of God! And I need your help to save my wife!"

"Yeah! Well, we're going to handcuff you and sit you on the curb until we get more information on the drugs."

"Hey man! Are you going to call the fire department for help? My wife's inside!"

Race-soldier Peter LaBlock replied, "Calm down! We're getting them now!"

Kenny Brown responded with, "Dear God, have mercy!"

Instead of destroying the front door and entering without announcement, they had decided to use a flash grenade, tossing it through the living room window. The device sparked a fire to the couch and carpet. It destroyed the house, killing Sharon in the blaze. Kenny Brown, the pastor of Faithful Truth Church of God and Christ, managed to escape with his life, leaving the First Lady of the church, Sharon Brown, behind.

Race-soldier Edward Shaw told LaBlock, "Got damn it LaBlock! I think we fucked up on this one."

"Fuck it Shaw! We'll write it up as mistaken identity. Hell! Maybe a mix-up in address! We'll clean it up! And make it stick."

The police found no drugs or weapons in the house. The race-soldiers were acting only on a hunch that the Browns were selling drugs, due to the fine expensive Cadillac cars in the driveway.

They had lied about drug transactions happening at the house in order to obtain a no-knock warrant for the raid. They subsequently wrote it up as a mistaken identity, perhaps a mix-up in address. Edward Shaw and Peter LaBlock were cleared of any wrongdoing in the process of an investigation. The device that caused the death of Sharon Brown was used by the race-soldiers against African American citizens on a daily basis. And it was used against people who were suspects on a mere hunch.

Chapter 5

Atrocities Against African Americans

For days, weeks and months, Chief Campbell and Mark Koon continued to push the idea of criminalizing the people's passion. Police conflicts were increasing in every part of south-central, giving the police a so-called legitimate reason to fill up the jails. As a result of their unscrupulous tactics, young Black males and females were being stopped, frisked, and arrested. Some were simply harassed for having their boom box music too loud, or for just hanging out on the streets. Others for standing in front of the corner store with their pants sagging below their waist. It was interactions like this that led to ongoing imprisonment because of bogus gun and drug charges.

In particular, one situation involved Mark Koon, in which a gun was found during a suspicious pedestrian stop. Mark falsely accused Henry Robinson of tossing a handgun in the bushes once he was spotted. Mark detained him, and walked over to a bush, claiming to have retrieved a handgun. Robinson was arrested and held in custody. He awaited trial for more than four months. The public defender requested a speedy trial and the prosecutor offered Robinson a plea deal. One year in prison with one year of probation. Robinson turned down the plea deal and asked his public defender to request evidence or fingerprints proving the gun belonged to him. He maintained his innocence because he knew that the gun did not belong to him. Robinson was subsequently acquitted on the gun charges. The following month, Robinson wanted compensation for the time he spent in jail on false charges. He sued the officer and the department, along with the city. During the time of the suit, Robinson died in a mysterious bus incident while waiting for the bus. Therefore, the lawsuit was dropped.

Edward Shaw, one of the race-soldiers, was on solo patrol and on the prowl, looking for someone – anyone – to arrest, and for anything. He spotted Cynthia Miles, a 16-year-old high school girl walking home from school.

"Reee Reee" (Car Siren)

"Stop! Freeze! Don't you try to run! You little Black bitch! Drop the books!"

"I'm not running anywhere! I didn't do anything."

"Did I tell you to speak?"

"No!"

"So, what the fuck are you talking for?"

"I'm just!"

"If you say one more thing! I'm going to put this nightstick down your fucking throat! Now! Give me your ID."

"I don't have any ID."

Shaw struck her with his night stick (Thump! Thump! Thump!)" I told you! I told you not to speak!"

"Ouch! Ouch! Officer! I didn't do anything! Why you hit me? I want your badge number! Give me your badge number!"

"Now you're going to jail! Get on your knees! Get on your knees! Smart-ass!"

"Hey Officer! I'm fucking bleeding! Sir!"

"Yeah! You should've shut the fuck up! Now you're going to jail!"

"Hey these cuffs hurt! Hey Officer! These cuffs are too tight!"

"Shut up nigger bitch!"

"These cuffs are too tight! You arresting me for no reason Officer!"

"I'll find something to pin on your ass! So, shut the fuck up!"

Officer Shaw took Cynthia Miles to jail for combative behavior on a police officer. She was only detained for a few hours and then released without any charges being filed against her. Her mother was called to pick her up later that evening.

Due to the lack of educational skills and/or in many cases, ignorance of the law, young Black men and women were being targeted and taken advantage of by the powers that be. Many of the citizens were shot and killed by nefarious cop behavior with impunity.

Chief Campbell began to reward the behavior of the race-soldiers, thinking they were doing noble deeds. His name was plastered all over the news media. The media collected their information from police reports, trusting that the information in them was true. Face it; falsifying a police report is a major offense, so why question it. The media praised Chief Campbell and ignored the cries of the people.

When the community was at the mercy of the police, Chief Campbell had a private conversation with Mark.

"Mark, have I told you lately what a wonderful job you guys are doing out there on those streets?"

"Well, sir! We aim to please and pleased to aim at anyone that stands in our way! That's what we're here for. We're going to take this country back to the way it used to be. Like the good old days."

"That's what I want to hear! Now, if we can get the other officers on board!"

"I'm sure we can get them on board! Me and my boys have ways of getting their cooperation."

"Do what you have to do out there! I'm looking real good for the next election, and I owe it all to you boys. You boys really know what it means to dominate."

"Yes Sir! We do our best."

"Don't you fellas let up."

"Sure thing, sir!"

"You're dismissed."

Mark Koon and his race-soldiers were shooting and killing people in the community as onlookers stood by. Those who witnessed the wrongdoing were always willing to testify against the race-soldiers, only to be disappointed due to witness tampering and obstruction of justice by the race-soldiers. Therefore, they ended up being acquitted with the help of police union appointed lawyers. The court system did not see the shooting and killing of unarmed citizens as systemic. It had gotten to the point that the justice system was blatantly failing the Black community. They turned a blind eye on a lot of questionable conflicts. Mark's clique was always set free with impunity for crimes against humanity.

My mother called me one night after watching the evening news. She wanted to express her concerns about what was going on in the city with the police shootings and killings, and with crimes against humanity in our community. She schooled me on some American history and atrocities against African Americans of many years ago that had been taught to her and passed down from her parents.

She first told me about the massacre of African Americans in Elaine, Arkansas, between September 30 and October 1, 1919

"Son, many years ago a band of white boys shot into a Black church. Black guards returned fire in order to defend and protect those who were in attendance at the church that day, and during the exchange a white guy was struck and killed. White folks claimed a Black insurrection. Soon, mobs of white folks, many of them deputized and given weapons by the city officials and law enforcement, attacked Blacks and massacred them."

I had to ask her how many of the people died.

"Son, there were about 237 Black people who died during that atrocity."

"Wow, it's very sad that our people had to go through that."

"Yeah, son, but that was not the only time. Let me tell you about the others."

She told me about the Wilmington, North Carolina massacre on African Americans in 1898, when a group of men said to be white supremacists conspired and led a mob of about 2,000 to overthrow the government.

They started with the Black citizens. They tried to start a civil war by destroying their property and killing between 60 and 300 Black people. The local officials stepped in and put a stop to it without punishment to the culprits. It was later found out that the mob largely responsible for the massacre were local white businessmen whose competitors were Black businessmen."

I was dumbfounded and heartbroken at the same time. I couldn't believe what I was hearing. She continued with the story of the Tulsa massacre that took place on May 31st and June 1, 1921, all because a Black elevator operator stumbled into a white woman while operating the elevator. She yelled rape and all hell broke loose with white men. They heard about the alleged incident and immediately the elevator operator was hauled off to jail, with allegations of attempted rape of a white woman. Local Black men ran to his defense once they found out that the Black fella had been jailed. White men began to break into the jail to retrieve the Black man for a lynching. Once again, the white residents were deputized and given weapons with the help of the U.S. government. Attacking the Black citizens from the ground and in aircraft, they destroyed the whole Black residential and business district of Greenwood in Tulsa, Oklahoma.

She spoke about the Rosewood massacre that occurred in the first week of January 1923 when a white woman claimed a Black man beat and raped her. It was later found out that it was her abusive secret lover. She was raped and battered by her lover but could not tell anyone. So, she blamed a Black man of the abuse, causing her husband to solicit help from every white man in town to join him and hunt down just about every Black man in Rosewood. This led to the killing and burning down of many homes and businesses of Black people. destroying the entire community.

My mother had me on the phone all night. I didn't grow tired of her history lesson. I actually wanted to hear more. However, I could not believe the action that our government took on handling those atrocities on American citizens.

"So, son, that's my concern on the way things are going in this community, and I never want that to happen here."

"Yes, Mom. I understand where you are coming from."

"Well son, I'm going to let you go for now so that you can get some sleep."

"Okay Mom. I'll talk with you later. Good night"

"Good night, son. I love you."

"I love you too."

The next day, a small group of citizens gathered together to protest in front of the police department. They began shouting and chanting with picket signs, marching in small circles.

"Hey man! We need some justice! I'm ready to shoot these cops back!"

"Yeah man! They're a bunch of pigs!! Let's find out where they live!"

"Man, they killing us and getting off! This shit has to stop!"

"Man, we should burn the police station down tonight! I'm fucking mad man!!"

"No justice! No peace! No justice! No peace! Fuck the police!"

A large part of the community took to protest. They had succumbed to a mob mentality and were ready to riot, which led to civil unrest and ended with the local pastors and clergymen cutting a deal with the mayor behind closed doors when the department heads would not reprimand Chief Campbell. In all of the shootings and killings by officers that were clearly wrong, the families of the victims were given large monetary settlements through court proceedings in place of real justice. Having their loved ones killed had become a constant routine.

Channel 7's news media anchor, Alex, started to cruise the community in his news van to interview the citizens for a good news story.

"Hey guy, I'm Alex with Channel 7 News. Would you like to express your feelings about the current events that are happening in your community?"

"Yeah man! My name is Larry, and I'd like to say they are going to bankrupt the city, giving these grieving families all that money! Lock up the cops! Lock up the cops! Lock up the cops! Racist! Racist! Racist cops! Stop the racist cops! Lock up the cops! Take away their pensions. Lock up the cops! Take away their pensions!"

"Thank you, for your opinion. I'm Alex, signing off with Channel 7 News."

Mark and the race-soldiers were patrolling Los Angeles like gods with badges, with Chief Campbell on their side. They began to change their targets to the more working-class Blacks in the community. The Black people who posed the greatest threat to them were the ones who pursued happiness and liberty — people with drive, ambition, and aspiration; the ones who had the ability to achieve. Black resilience and Black resolve were being punished and justified by law and conflict. It was counterintuitive to what this country was built on. On many occasions the race-soldiers would go out of their way to show disrespect to a lot of the well-to-do citizens.

For instance, Mr. Robinson, a Black business owner, dressed in a suit and tie, driving his brand-new Mercedes Benz, was mistaken for an alleged robbery suspect. Race-soldier Chad Miller pulled him over and made him sit on the curb in his suit. The officer held Robinson at gunpoint as he sat on the curb near the squad car until the radio dispatcher returned information, describing Robinson as a well-known businessman with no criminal record.

With a confused look on his face Mr. Robinson uttered, *"Good afternoon, Officer."*

"Is this your car? Let me see your license and registration. Move slowly and keep your hands where I can see them."

"Yes, it is sir! What's the problem, Officer? Why am I being stopped?"

"Where did you get this car? And you definitely fit the description of someone we're looking for."

"Sir, I'm on the way to work! I didn't do anything, and I bought this car yesterday!"

"Just give me your license and registration. Keep your hands where I see them!"

"Yes, sir! Here you go!"

"Stay here! And shut up!"

"Okay."

"Now, step out the car! And put your hands-on top of your head! I want you to sit over there on the curb while I run your information! Don't make any fast moves!"

"Yes sir!"

"All right! Everything checks out! You're free to go!"

I became more aware of many of these situations when we would get a dispatch call to all units in the area. As I arrived on the scene, I would witness what would sometimes be mind-bending for me because I did not have the wherewithal to do or say anything due to the blue wall of silence. The "blue wall of silence" rule assured officers that, as a show of loyalty, other fellow officers would not interfere with police abuse or testify against each other. However, I had taken an oath, and therefore, I felt chaos lurking around the corner; their behavior was uninhibited.

I had to have a talk with my partner, Officer O'Malley, about my feelings with dealing with Mark and the race-soldiers. I needed to find a way to blow the whistle on those guys.

"Hey O'Malley. Man, I'm ready to go talk to the Chief about Mark and those race-soldiers."

"Hey man! Do you think that's a good idea? And why do you call them race-soldiers anyway?"

"Because back in the day when I was in the military, I was informed about those guys. After a night on the town I had a conflict with those same guys. They targeted Black people and mistreated them. They believe in white supremacy and from what I've seen and heard I believe it. Yeah! I'm profoundly affected by the reality of my race in this city! Those cops are a menace to society."

"I hear you man. If you feel that strongly about it! Go in and talk to the Chief. But I tell you, he is a hard nut to crack."

I went to Chief Campbell. At this point he was beyond reproach. I tried to have somewhat of a real heart-to-heart about Mark and the race-soldiers while they were patrolling the community and what they were doing to the community. In order to make me go away, he gave me a $50.00 raise.

"Chief Campbell, I need to have a word with you."

"What is it this time, Smith?"

"Well, it's about Mark and those other fellows."

"Look Smith! I don't want to hear shit about those men!"

"But sir!"

"But my ass! Leave it alone, Smith!"

"Yeah! Okay Chief!"

"Hey Smith! Are you still working that second job?"

"Yes why?"

"Well look here, I'm going to look into getting you a pay increase. I'm talking about $50.00 more."

"Hey thanks, Chief!"

"But remember what I said! Leave Mark and those fellas alone!"

"Yeah, but they need to simmer down".

"Got damn it Smith! You want the money or not?"

I accepted the pay increase and no longer had to take on a second job. The increase in pay was great, but at the same time I felt like I was selling my people out. I was treating my community unjustly and was doing a disservice to them as conformity was pushed. I needed to deal with my conscience as bigotry and racism were on the rise. I kept reflecting on the stories my mother had told me about the African American communities. I thought of the years before and knew in my heart that I would never want that to ever happen again.

This one evening when Amy and I were out on one of our weekend dates, Mark spotted us as he was on patrol with Edward Shaw. They had a stare like I've seen before. It was the same exact expression I got from them back in the day when I wanted to have some fun with Tabitha in the whorehouse! I had to ask Amy "Did you see that look?"

Amy responded adamantly "Yeah, I told you that some of these officers were weird!"

I let Amy know that I was not comfortable with it.

"They gave us the look of hatred and disapproval."

Monday morning came around, and out of nowhere, the order came from Chief Campbell that Amy was being transferred from riding and patrolling with her old partner to having to work with one of Mark's race-soldiers, Ernest Clinton. Someone must have gotten the message to the Chief.

I got the impression that neither Chief Campbell nor Mark and the race-soldiers liked the idea of me being with a white woman, and I didn't give a damn. I didn't like the idea of them killing and hurting my people. They were always in good standing with the chief, it was a strange relationship and I really couldn't figure it out. The thought of Chief Campbell being a racist crossed my mind on several occasions, as I watched how he would not reprimand any of the race-soldiers on questionable behavior, but officers who were not a part of the group were often written up or chastised by the chief for their actions out in the field.

I knew this would not be a good thing, but with Amy being a brilliant lady with her educational background as a civil rights attorney, she would often venture into subtle investigations into Mark and his race-soldiers while working alongside of them. She would pick his brain and collect dates, times, who, what, where, and how. She befriended the race-soldiers and shared all the information with me. I stored every bit of it, thinking that it might one day be used in RICO law charges to prosecute individuals who engage in organized crime. In 1970, Congress passed the Racketeer Influenced and Corrupt Organizations law, which is called the RICO law.

"So, how long have you been in law enforcement?"

"Well, we as a group have been fighting for America's beliefs all our lives!"

"So, you guys came to the department as a group?"

"Yeah, we're a team! We enforce law and order the American way!"

At this point, the race-soldiers were acting like an organization within the police department, doing their best to uphold the status quo of the system and declaring war on the citizens of the African American community under the color of law. It's a crime for one or more using the power allowed to them by a governmental agency to deprive or conspire willfully to deprive another person of any rights that are protected by the Constitution or laws of the United States.

They were working on a racist agenda to hold back a race of people, no matter what the cost, with the thought in mind that the end justifies the means. Giving a good outcome would excuse their bad deeds, and the crimes they were committing on the Black community would be in their favor. Their white supremacy agenda was in full swing and Chief Campbell was looking good in the election race. The media was having a field day reporting manufactured arrests supporting a war on crime.

Chapter 6

Ms. Benson's Boys

It was Christmas Eve. Gregory and Teddy were returning home from Bible study and choir rehearsal. As soon as they drove off the church's parking lot, race-soldier, Officer Clinton, commanded Officer Freeman to hit the lights and sirens and order the driver to pull over. They hadn't come to a complete stop before he started releasing his seatbelt and exiting the squad car. With his gun drawn, Officer Clinton cautiously approached the passenger side of the vehicle. He began to give orders and commands.

"Driver put your hands where I can see them! Passenger put your hands outside of the car! Don't make any sudden moves; I'll blow your fucking head off!"

With Teddy being the youngest, and never having experienced any hostile police behavior, he was confused and frightened. He was so nervous that he wet his pants, he confessed to Gregory.

"Greg, I'm scared. What am I supposed to do?"

Gregory tried to comfort him.

"Teddy, just do whatever he says. Don't give him any reason to shoot us. Just be cool and I'll handle it."

Gregory rolled down the window.

"Good evening Officer. Can you tell me what I'm being pulled over for?"

That is when Officer Clinton explained his claim.

"We got a call looking for two Black guys that just robbed a bank! You guys rob a bank?"

Gregory denied having anything to do with a robbery.

"No! At this time of night? We just came from that church right over there!"

Gregory, being the eldest and protector of his younger brother, picked up the Bible to explain to Officer Clinton how it was impossible for the two of them to be the suspects. "We just left church praising the Lord and singing praises. The people there can vouch for us."

Gregory began to wave the Bible around and proceeded to hand it over to Officer Clinton, reaching across Teddy. Officer Amy Freeman approached the driver's side of the two-seater sports car with her flashlight shining it through the window. She then requested to see his license and registration.

"Good evening gentlemen. May I see your license and registration, please?"

Gregory, following the officer's request, reached for his license and registration and handed it to her.

"Sure, no problem. Here you go."

Amy collected the information and went back to the squad car.

"Thank you! I'll be right back."

She calmly walked over to the squad car to run the plate to check for any outstanding warrants. Thinking the situation was under control, she ran the license plate and the driver's information. She kept an eye on her partner, watching through the windshield of the squad car. While waiting for the dispatcher to return the information, Officer Clinton continued to question the two young men. Suddenly, and out of nowhere, his anger escalated beyond control

Officer Clinton yelled, "Gun!!"

He began to discharge his weapon indiscriminately and recklessly into the classic Porsche, striking both the driver and passenger several times.

"Radio to headquarters! Come in headquarters! This is Officer Clinton! Come in!"

"This is headquarters, what are you reporting?"

"I have shots fired! Officer involved shooting at 60th and Broadway! Send medical attention and back up!"

"10-4. Units are on the way with medical assistance!"

Teddy was hit several times, as bullets ripped through his head and shoulder. He had no chance of coming out alive; he was dead. Gregory was hit twice, one bullet entered the base of his skull and the other, through his neck. His body writhing and blood oozing out of the side his neck and head. Clinton then proceeded to run back to the squad car and leave the Porsche a bloody scene. He immediately began making accusations, blaming Gregory and Teddy for the shooting. The race-soldier came up with a convoluted story stating he mistook a book for a gun and he feared for his life. This was an attempt to justify the shooting.

Later that evening, my mother's friend, Ms. Benson, received a call from Johnny, a neighborhood watch member, stating that her sons Gregory and Teddy had been shot during a routine traffic stop.

"Ms. Benson!"

"Yes."

"You need to get down here."

"Get down where? Who is this and what's going on?"

"This is Johnny from down the street. The police just shot your two sons!"

"Shot! Lord Jesus. Where are they?"

"They're on 60th and Broadway."

"I'm on my way! Let me call my friend!"

Ms. Benson immediately phoned my mother to give her a ride to where the incident had taken place. My mother rushed over to Ms. Benson's home and they proceeded to the scene. Once at the scene, yellow caution tape was used as a barrier between the onlookers and the horrific scene. Ms. Benson immediately exited the car and attempted to charge through the barrier only to be stopped and embraced by Amy. Whispering words of compassion and grief, Amy tried to comfort and console Ms. Benson. Once medical assistance and the coroner removed the deceased and wounded, my mother quietly drove Ms. Benson back to her home. She expressed solace to give her strength for the days to come. My mother went home and made calls to gather all the members of the Neighborhood Watch committee. She also summoned me by telephone to come and join the discussion they were having about the shooting.

"Robert, we have to do something about all of these unwarranted shootings! These cops are going crazy, killing all our young men. If this keeps up, they'll all be dead. We need to talk about a strategy to get these crooked cops off our streets. They just shot Ms. Benson's boys! I need you to get over here as soon as possible!"

"I'm in; I'll be right over!"

As I was gearing up to go meet with my mother and her committee, I received a phone call from Amy.

"Hello."

"Hey Robert, this is Amy."

"What's going on, Amy? You sound upset; is everything okay?"

"Me and my partner were just involved in a shooting, and it looks bad. I'll tell you about it later."

"Oh, yeah? My mother's friend's sons were just shot, too!"

"Oh, Robert it might be them!"

"Okay, I'm heading over to my mom's now. I'll talk to you when we get home. Be safe out there."

"Okay, I will."

We met up at my mother's home and offered Ms. Benson our condolences. The meeting was brief and sorrowful, and we planned to meet again the next week. We all agreed to help Ms. Benson with funeral costs and hospital bills for the two young men. We needed to come together as a community.

Hours later, Amy had to provide an unbiased statement on what she actually saw.

Amy's report:

As we spotted the yellow classic 1968 Porsche 911 in the vicinity of 60th Street and Broadway Place, the two occupants inside were ordered to pull over to the curb and show their hands. All occupants complied with the orders. As things appeared clear of danger, I approached on the driver's side and requested to see the driver's license and registration. I was given the documents and preceded back to my squad car to run a make on the vehicle and the driver. During my call I had a view of Officer Clinton having an exchange with the occupants. In a matter of seconds, I witnessed Officer Clinton's stable behavior switch to an enraged behavior. He began to discharge his weapon indiscriminately into the occupants' vehicle, wounding all occupants.

Amy's account of the situation was overridden by what Officer Clinton claims he felt at the time of the shooting. Because of what Amy reported in her statement regarding the incident involving Officer Clinton, she came under harsh scrutiny by over half of the department. Many of the officers did not speak to her and did not want to work with her.

"We heard what you told our superiors about the incident".

"I told them what happened. What's the big deal?"

"Just know that we're watching you and we don't trust you. So much for the blue code! When it comes to you Amy, you crossed the blue line. You're a snitch and a rat. Blood in, Blood out, Amy"

Amy's so-called fellow cops were basically telling her is that once you're in here, you die here. What goes on in the department stays in the department. They didn't like Amy going against Clinton's reporting. The blue code or the Code of Silence is common throughout the nation. About 79% of law enforcement believes in the code. The code is used mostly when it comes to excessive force that involves a citizen who's been abused or killed.

She was assigned to desk duty while her partner was placed on leave with pay. He took a vacation until Internal Affairs began an investigation into the discrepancies of the two officers' reports.

In the days to come, my mother and her friends collected money from every direction. They sought help from church pastors, street pimps, street hustlers, and gangbangers. They all pitched in to help raise enough money to bury Teddy and take care of the hospital bills for Gregory, who had survived.

As they began to search for legal representation on behalf of Ms. Benson's boys, my mother and Ms. Benson made it clear to me that it was time to galvanize the Black folks in the community. It was time to fight back and live! That really put Amy and me in a very difficult and dangerous situation because we were both police officers. The entire community knew that Ms. Benson's sons were really good boys, the salt of the earth kind of guys, and enough was enough.

We had to get a handle on this situation. Not only that; things were also getting out of hand with a few of my fellow officers. It was hitting really close to home. People I actually knew were dying at the hands of these rogue officers. These were the same guys who beat me in the military.

Teddy's funeral was held at Greater Hope Baptist Church in south-central on 81st and Figueroa, with a host of friends and family in attendance. Pastor Eugene Wright delivered the eulogy. Teddy's body was later taken to Inglewood Cemetery to its final resting place. Days after Teddy's funeral a few of the community members met up again. My mother's home was the meeting place. We had to discuss a deeper strategy. To my surprise, my Uncle Conrad was there, sitting at the dinner table. He was waiting for the meeting to get started.

My mother entered the house with Ms. Benson and examined the room and greeted everyone.

"I'm glad to see everyone here. We're gathered here today to reach an agreement. We need to find a solution on how to handle these cops! Everyone knows Ms. Benson's boys were shot two weeks ago. I asked my brother Conrad to join us in the fight. Conrad, is there anything you want to say?"

Conrad stood up looking around the room and began to speak.

"Yes, Mary. I want to tell everyone that I'm here to help in any way I can. I've been ready to fight these racist pigs for a long time! It's time for some compensation! Payback is a bitch! That's all I have to say!"

She then turned to me:

"Robert, do you have anything to say?"

"Well, I'm here to give my best support. and I'm in agreement with Uncle Conrad."

Once I had my say, she then proceeded to address the entire group.

"We're going to need all hands on deck! We have to go out to the community and solicit everyone's help with fighting back. We are going to make sure our community is safe and it's by any means necessary. If we have to file lawsuits and take down badge numbers, then that's what we'll do. If you see something say something. This is not the time to be a silent partner. We need gang members, good cops, and common people to join in the fight. We are going to continue to meet up and discuss fighting back. So, for now, I would like everyone to go out and do some kind of recruiting, and we'll keep in touch."

When the meeting ended, I was sitting at the dinner table with my Uncle Conrad. He explained to me why he was a Vietnam Veteran who lived with a chip on his shoulder. He was like a walking encyclopedia. He had a revolutionary mind. He would tell me stories and go on forever. His stories were based on his experience with the war and losing his daughter at the hands of law enforcement. He also resented the way he was treated in his country after the war. He told me that the Vietnam War was the first war in which its American troops were fully integrated. It was a development that was supposed to turn the page on an unjust history of institutional racism in the military. He felt the Black troops were discriminated against, although they were fighting the same war. Many of the white soldiers had deep southern racist roots; they took the Jim Crow ideas with them. Those structures persisted overseas, even while Black and white soldiers had to fight side-by-side. When he was in Saigon, he would often spend his time off in a section of the city called Soul Ville. Segregation was still a way of life. Meanwhile, white soldiers were being promoted at a higher rate. He thought he would be treated like a king, but instead he felt like a pawn.

He told me the story of how my cousin was, as he described it, murdered at the hands of law enforcement. After the summer of 1967, she was traveling back to school when a highway trooper stopped her for a wrongful lane change. Words were exchanged and the trooper decided to arrest her, charging her with disorderly conduct. While in police custody overnight, a deputy attempted to rape her in her cell. There was a struggle and he was kicked in the groin. He sucker-punched her, knocking her to the floor, blood gushing from her battered face. He beat her until the air left her body. It was labeled self-defense and an assault on a deputy.

"I tell you, young-blood, I don't give a fuck about this system of white supremacy! Those devils fucked me all through my life! They don't give a fuck about the people! Do you understand me, young-blood?"

"Yeah, I understand where you're coming from, Uncle."

Uncle Conrad continued to tell me his story, and about how he was exposed to Agent Orange.

"I mean, they treat their veterans like shit! They send you off to fight. Men were sprayed with that Agent Orange shit in so-called friendly fire. Then when you come back (if you come back!), they don't do anything to help you out of your situation! Man! I've been on medication ever since I've been back! And that's a long time, young blood! They use and abuse you, then forget about you. I lost my daughter to this system. Not to mention, they let that pig get away with killing my baby girl! I know you're in law enforcement, but I've been holding onto this shit for a long time, young blood! I'm ready to get it on!"

"I feel your pain, Uncle! We're going to handle it, one way or another. "

"Cool, young-blood."

The meeting was adjourned, and we agreed to continue to meet. Our morale was really building up on fighting back.

Chapter 7

My Gang Member Kinfolks

We had to come up with a plan and an understanding that we were going to join my mother's group. It was time to organize and take on a group of fellow officers who were not willing to uphold their pledge to their oath. We all knew that law enforcement had a strong defensive team to fight against the community. The police union was backing them, giving the community a slim chance of victory. Many of the parents of the deceased young men and women who had been insensibly murdered by the race-soldiers joined in to help make a change. More than half of the families had not come close to real justice, but instead, received big money checks. Lady Justice wears a blindfold, which represents impartiality without regard to wealth, power, or race. However, the citizens of the community did not share in those sentiments. Instead, they saw it as a misrepresentation of justice altogether.

A few of the citizens were marching with signs and protesting on the corner of Avalon and Imperial. They were shouting at the cars passing by.

"Hey, man! We are so tired of this shit! They are treating us like we don't matter!

One protester began telling the group, "Yeah! We really need to get our guns and fight back!"

Just then another protester in the group yelled out, "We are the only ones who can save us! This government doesn't give a shit about us!"

Another one chimed in, followed by another.

"We, as a people, have faced so many atrocities!"

"We must begin to fight this system!"

As the citizens began to galvanize and become more of a cohesive mechanism in the community, there were some do's and don'ts that needed to be in place to get on the same page to survive the wrath that was being cast upon our community. The gangs were embroiled in a street war. My mother took to the streets and recruited some of my gang member kinfolks and their friends. She recruited well over twenty gang members. Even though they were once rivals, they were able to set their differences aside and call a truce.

"We need you guys to get on the same page. You have to set the gangbanging aside; we really need your help!

One of the gang members spoke up.

"Hey! Why don't we just get those cops' addresses? You know what I mean?"

My mother replied, "We're going to have to strategize! Come up with a plan!"

I offered the gang members a second chance to do better and gave them something to really fight for in the community. They started to focus on the larger picture, realizing that the community must make an effort to help one another in order to survive. Unification was the only way to live among a group of bad and shady police officers who were justified by law and conflict. These bad apples had the full support of the Chief of Police.

My mother placed me and my Uncle Conrad in charge of training the gang members. I passed on all the knowledge that the Army had given me in combat fighting and weaponry training. I informed them about their civil rights on the streets, what the cops could and could not do to them.

Conrad began to address the gang members with his plans.

"I'm going to train you guys. I'll teach you how to really handle yourselves when it comes to dealing with the opposition!"

One of the gang members spoke up.

"Hey man! You're going to teach us that karate shit?"

Conrad felt he had to be direct with them.

"I'll teach you how get those racist guys' feet off your necks!"

Another gang member took another jab at Conrad.

"Are you going to teach us how to put a bullet in their asses?"

Once again Conrad came direct.

"I'll teach you how to fight the power!"

Many of the citizens who received big check payouts for wrongful deaths from the city provided the revenue for the training, weapons, and building space. We were able to secure a building located on Imperial and Avalon. That intersection is where the community gathered, organized, and held meetings. Before we could occupy the building, we had to rid the entire intersection of trash and debris left behind from the last gathering just days before. I agreed with my mother, that we had to establish a system outside of the department to effectively make sure that there would be accountability for the race-soldiers' actions.

My mother felt that she needed to have a heart-to-heart with me.

"Son, I need you to be careful! I know you're walking a fine line.

"Yeah, I'm watching my back. I have my eyes on those guys.

"How are you coming along with the neighborhood guys?

"They're really trying to learn the techniques. I explained their rights pertaining to the law."

"Okay, great!"

The community was gearing up to fight the power and become more of a force against whatever the race-soldiers were going to bring to community next. Ms. Benson still needed to retain a civil rights lawyer to file a case against the race-soldier who shot her two sons. That's when Amy thought that she could be of some help in the fight since she was a witness to the shooting. She made a call to her big brother, civil rights attorney and skillful prosecutor, Arthur Freeman. He was willing to take the case on pro bono. Attorney Arthur Freeman was the spitting image of Amy's father, but only younger.

He was a very tall, stern, redheaded gentleman with a kind spirit. Amy thought that she could work in close proximity to Arthur and at the same time remain in the background and give him pertinent information to the case.

"Hello. Hey I'm Attorney Freeman. I told Amy that I would be pleased to take on the fight."

Ms. Benson expressed her appreciation to Attorney Freeman.

"Great! I'm so thankful for your willingness to help. I appreciate you travelling so far; I know you had to come from Alabama."

"Yeah, I heard your boys were great young men."

Ms. Benson replied, "Yes, they are. We buried Teddy last week and Gregory is not doing too well."

"Ms. Benson, I'll do my best! We'll see what happens with the DA in the criminal case."

Internal Affairs concluded their investigation and determined that Amy's reported statement was not credible, therefore rendering the case closed. The case was later picked up by the state prosecutors office and moved on to a judicial court with the race-soldier on trial — the people of the state of California vs. Officer Ernest Clinton. The burden of proof was left to the people, which had to prove that the defendant acted in an unlawful manner.

The criminal trial was set and subsequently postponed and almost dismissed for the lack of evidence by the state. Chief Campbell continued to try different methods to prevent Amy from testifying against the race-soldier, who happened to be her former partner. Ms. Benson's son, Gregory, was incapacitated and was in no condition to testify due to the injuries he suffered to his spinal cord at the base of his skull. He lost complete vision in his right eye, his vocal cords were destroyed, which resulted him being in a quadriplegic state without speech. The race-soldier requested a speedy trial. A clause of the Sixth Amendment to the United States Constitution states that it provides that all prosecutions and the accused shall have the right to a speedy trial.

As the prosecuting attorneys scrambled to put on their case and began working with a lack of testimonies, the people still felt optimistic about prosecuting the race-soldier to the full extent of the law. The thought of the age-old obstacles of racism had often appeared when there was a case of Black vs. White in our great country of America. The fate of the race soldier would be up to twelve jurors of his peers.

The trial was moved to Torrance, California, a couple of cities over with a law-and-order type of feel in the city that was more favorable for officers. The trial lasted a little over two weeks, ending and resulting in a deadlock, with the possibility of a retrial. The jury was unable to establish the guilt of the race-soldier beyond a reasonable doubt. They were not able to determine if the officer acted outside of the law and if he violated the constitutional rights of the citizens in any criminal way. Although it was evident that the race-soldier pulled the trigger, they could not determine if law and conflict justified him. Ms. Benson was outraged about the outcome of the trial. Attorney Freeman tried to console her and restore her belief in the justice system.

Ms. Benson looked up at the sky and yelled with tears in her eyes, "I can't believe that cop got off! He killed my baby!"

"I'm sorry Ms. Benson! I'm very sorry! Let's see if we can get justice next time."

The feelings of defeat, depression, and melancholy began to smother the whole community. Their faces were distorted with anger with the thought of justice deferred and maybe justice denied. There was still a plan to build up a defense mechanism that would somehow put a stop to the killing and brutality by these rogue officers. The community was suffering once again.

My mother's goal was to direct the community's hope and ambitions toward achieving strength and resilience. She shared information about a community from many years ago, where the Black community's human rights were constantly violated. That community is where the self-defense policy was born with a gentleman by the name of Robert Williams, who said, "there is a need to meet violence with violence." Although he did not promote aggression — only self-defense, he made it clear to everyone that Black militants are not here to promote violence, but that they were simply combating it.

Uncle Conrad and I worked on the gang members and helped them to get rid of their gangbanger demeanor. They developed a more military tactical state of mind by respecting and protecting the community's citizens. We continued training and converting them into fearless street-soldiers, ready to protect the people by justified means. Uncle Conrad gave the street-soldiers a lesson on respecting and protecting the women in the community.

Conrad opened up the meeting giving the street-soldiers a lesson on Black women.

"Listen up young soldiers! They call me Conrad! I've been around a long time! And the main thing on this earth I cherish the most, is my Black sistas! Black women are to be loved and adored! Can you dig it?"

The group replied, "Yes sir!"

Conrad continued to speak. "I mean Black women are the mothers of this earth! All mankind comes from the Black woman. Can you dig it?"

The group replied, "Yes sir!"

Conrad continued to speak. "She needs to be protected by any means. Without her there is no us! Can you dig it!"

The group replied, "Yes sir!"

Conrad began to preach to the group. "We both are under the same struggle umbrella! Can you dig it!"

The group replied, "Yes sir!"

Conrad really got into orator mode.

"A revolution has to be thorough or else it's doomed! A real revolutionist knows that, which is why they have to proceed in cold blood! We want to change the world we living in, not just sit around talking about it. We gotta actually do something about it! That's how a true revolutionist get down, you dig?"

The group replied, "Yes sir!"

Conrad continued to lecture, "Okay men, you're no longer gang members; you're now street-soldiers!"

A group member replied, "Yeah! No problem! We will do a better job as protectors!"

Conrad replied, "Yes! Men, you are street-soldiers! Street-soldiers to stand shoulder to shoulder!"

A group member replied, "Yes! Sir! Sir, when are we going to get the guns?"

Conrad replied, "I need to work some things out first. I'm working on arming all you fellas."

The group replied, "Yes sir! That's what we need!"

Conrad replied, "I have to get you men ready for that first!"

Conrad continued to really drill the street-soldiers. He wanted to build their inner strength as soldiers. He told them that "a valiant soldier experiences death only once, but a coward has death a million times."

He became very devoted to training the street-soldiers to develop a courageous attitude on a daily basis. He began to teach them how to humble themselves, handle their grief, and manage their rage. He was building them to become real street-soldiers. He began to tell them about the sacrifices a soldier has to make when protecting the community and about the higher purpose in defending the people.

Justified by Law and Conflict

Chapter 8

Monetary Award

Because of a deadlock in the criminal case, a jury of eight white men, two Asian American women, and two white women in the city of Torrance, California, was not able to find the race-soldier guilty of killing and wounding Ms. Benson's boys. Ms. Benson was then able to proceed with a civil case against the race-soldier.

Attorney Freeman went to work right away. He needed to determine if excessive force was used in the killing of Teddy. Because it's virtually impossible to get into the mind of a person, Attorney Freeman was faced with the difficult task of determining the intention and motivation surrounding facts and circumstances that led to the use of excessive force. In a civil lawsuit, the plaintiff must establish the defendant's liability only according to the preponderance of evidence and the defendants are not entitled to the same legal protections. Ms. Benson understood that if she won the case on behalf of her sons, it would not be a criminal conviction; it would only be a punishment that consisted of a monetary award.

The case lasted for five consecutive days as the judge established the race-soldier's liability for the death and injuries of Teddy and Gregory Benson. During the trial, several witnesses were called and loads of evidence was presented. As it turned out, Amy's statement was the key that led Ms. Benson to victory. Ms. Benson fell to her knees and raised her arms to the sky and yelled, "Hallelujah! Hallelujah! God is good! Lord have mercy! My son's life was not in vain!"

Ms. Benson was awarded two million dollars, which was paid out by the City of Los Angeles. While the police union protects the police from investigation and prosecution stemming from their conduct, this time they did not prevail. Ms. Benson expressed to Attorney Freeman how forever grateful she was for taking on the case on behalf of her sons. She said that she would give her life in place of her sons, which no amount of money can replace.

"I'm still not satisfied with this! I want to put that devil away! I will continue to fight until my very last breath! My sons were not the first Black men to be victims of this broken system, and I'm sure they won't be the last. So, we must continue the fight!"

Ms. Benson made a vow to spend the majority of the money awarded to her for the loss of her sons to help to fight against the race-soldiers. She began conducting legal investigations to help get them off the streets through justified by law or even conflict.

Days after the verdict, my mother gave Ms. Benson a small victory celebration at the community building where the community meetings were held. There was a crowd of about 20 people from the community with refreshments and a disc jockey, and a group of the street-soldiers that stood outside for their security and protection. I was in attendance, along with Amy and her brother, Attorney Freeman, just before he was to take flight to return back to his home in Alabama. I had to find out if my mother blessed the gathering crowd with some of her southern cooking, so I approached her in an almost begging tone when I asked her about the smothered pork chops.

"Momma, did you make some of your smothered pork chops?"

She came with a reply I didn't expect. "No, I thought that Amy would bring some of hers!"

"But I have missed your cooking for a while."

"Oh no! I was looking forward to some of yours!"

She wasn't concerned about my cravings. "There's a lot of food in there. Go get some!"

As the event got underway, the crowd expressed their adulation to Attorney Freeman for the work he had done on the case. Everyone was having a great time and beginning to really enjoy themselves. My mother was raising her cup to make a speech, and folks were dancing around rejoicing.

The DJ was playing a James Brown tune, "The Big Pay Back," when one of the young street-soldiers burst into the door with his face a bloody mess. He yelled out to the crowd, "Hey y'all! They're out there beating on Kevin!"

Somebody in the crowd yelled back, "Who's out there?"

The bloody street-soldier replied, "Those bad cops!"

My mother said, "Aww wow! Let's go see! C'mon! C'mon!"

He struggled to inform the crowd that Mark and the race-soldiers were outside in a confrontation with the street-soldiers. Everyone started running to see exactly what was going on. By the time Amy and I made it out front where the conflict was taking place, Mark was beating a street-soldier. We could hear him saying, "Stop resisting!" as he was hitting him with his nightstick. He was stomping and kicking him with his big black steel-toed boots on the ground, rendering him unconscious.

"Where's your got damn ID, boy? You hear me talking to you boy? Where's your ID?"

I could see that Mark was being overly aggressive and out of control, so I placed my right hand on my service revolver, I unsnapped the holster and cocked back the hammer, and yelled out an order to Mark.

"Mark! Mark! Let him up! Lay up off of him!"

Mark countered by badgering the street-soldier. "Where's your got damn ID, boy!"

I pulled my service revolver and pointed it at Mark and said, "Lay off, Mark!"

As the street-soldier lay on the sidewalk, Mark was requesting to see his identification. At the same time, all the other street-soldiers stood by at gunpoint from the other race-soldiers.

When I yelled at Mark to let up off the street-soldier, he acted as if he didn't hear me. As I proceeded to approach him with my gun in hand, one of the race-soldiers pointed his service revolver toward me, so Amy drew her service revolver on him. It was a show down right at the intersection of Imperial and Avalon. Mark looked at me and spoke.

"Oh! It's like that?"

I looked him in his eyes and said, "Yeah! It's like that! You're trying to kill him?"

Mark replied, "Yeah! I just might!"

Mark removed his revolver and yelled Get up DAN!! And go home!!

I yelled out to the street-soldiers, "Y'all help him up, please! Get him some medical attention."

A group of street-soldiers helped him to his feet.

Mark turned around, looked at the crowd and yelled, "What are y'all looking at? Clear out!! Bobby! Bobby! The Negro hero!"

It looked like something out of a western movie. More of the community began to gather as witnesses. My mother, Ms. Benson, and Attorney Freeman watched from afar. Mark had no intention of arresting the guy; he just wanted to make certain that his authoritarian presence was felt.

It seemed like something right out of the playbook of the antebellum south. That was when whites held all the power with authority, when Africans were forced here to America by the shiploads and made to perform slave duties. Africans made America profitable. In South Carolina, Africans vastly outnumbered whites. White South Carolinians became concerned and adopted a slave code. The code gave groups of white, armed men, who were hired, the civic duties of keeping the Africans in order, preventing them from revolting by striking fear into their very souls.

Amy and I decided to really invest our time into investigating Mark and the race-soldiers from the inside. Mark and the race-soldiers were acting as a gang within the department. Anyone who spoke out against bad cops was targeted as a citizen against the whole country. They were staunch defenders of their bad practices. They wore tattoos of the confederate flag on their right arm, and the American flag on the left arm. They were a gang of officers that believed in fighting for the Confederacy before fighting for the beliefs of the American way of life. However, they believed the American way of life was theirs and theirs alone. Their conduct, in many cases, was reprehensible and designed to exact fear in the community.

Mark and I were back to the old military days of being on different sides of the track as adversaries. As soon as I got back to the precinct, the chief chewed my ass out for so-called interfering with police duties. When he called me into his office, I thought that I would get my chance to air my grievances.

"Hey Chief, I need to have a word with you again. I need to file a complaint." Sitting behind his desk, he threw his pencil down, leaned back in his chair with an irritating frown on his face.

"This is the third time! What is it about now, Smith?"

I began to complain about the race-soldiers' behavior.

"About Mark and that crew of lawless cop friends of his."

Chief Campbell stopped me mid-sentence and began to defend them.

"I thought we had this talk before Smith. Those guys are off-limits. Why are you in my office complaining about your fellow officers?"

I tried to get a word in.

"Hey Chief, I'm just saying, the things those guys are doing are not fair to the community."

The chief grew angry with me and started shouting.

"I say what's fair in those streets! You just stay in line! Never mind those guys!"

I was trying to tell the chief that I was a good officer seeing bad officers doing wrong.

"Sir! I took an oath!"

His reply was shocking to me.

"Your oath has nothing to do with those guys!"

So, I saw that I wasn't getting anywhere with him.

"Am I dismissed?"

He was pleased to get rid of me.

"Yes! You're dismissed!"

I attempted to file a complaint against Mark about his abusive tactics and the gross misconduct that went on unexamined. I just could not figure out why the chief was so protective of Mark and the race-soldiers as they played by their own set of rules.

I grew very determined to get Mark and the race-soldiers thrown off the Los Angeles police force. Even if it took every ounce of my being, I was willing to risk it all.

Chapter 9

My Romantic Side

I had begun to display a lot of pent-up frustration due to the havoc Mark and the race-soldiers were wreaking on the community. My professional life was overriding what was best for my personal life. I took time off my busy life and decided to bring home flowers for Amy and share my romantic side with her. As soon as I came in the house, Amy said, "Aww! You shouldn't have!"

"Yeah, I thought I needed to bring you some flowers."

"They're beautiful! I love your romantic heart."

"I told you, I was your man!"

"Yes! Give me a kiss!"

As Amy and I managed to search for a little bit of romance in our relationship, we would surprise one another with romantic flowers and gifts after a long hard week of work. The workload would intensify the lovemaking in a more passionate and erotic way throughout the evening, to our satisfaction.

We would sometimes get into brief quarrels about Mark and how he should be handled, since we could not get any help or support from Chief Campbell. Amy suggested that we have the department wiretapped. But in order to do that, we needed to follow protocol.

"You know, if we could wiretap the department, it would probably help us out."

"Yeah, but you know what we would have to go through?"

"I don't know if we can really trust all that's involved."

"Yeah, we need to come up with some information on these characters."

First, we would have to summon the FBI as the federal agent would need to get the permission of a judge to tap the phone line of the department. The way things were going in the department, we really did not know if we could trust the outcome.

Amy returned to work Monday morning and went right to work trying to figure out exactly what was going on between Mark and Chief Campbell. Amy performed her regular desk duties in order not to raise suspicion about her secret mission to investigate Mark and Chief Campbell. While Chief Campbell was out of his office she prowled through his desk before canvassing the file cabinet.

Amy came across something and thought to herself, "What could this be? I need to look into this. Something's not right."

She discovered photocopied payroll checks in her quest to seek information, with 'Mark Koon Incorporated' printed on them. The payroll checks seemed to be the linchpin in our private investigation as it took an incredible turn.

"Arthur, I need you to check this out for me. Run some background to find the paper trail."

"Okay Amy, I'm on it."

"Hey thank you brother! I love you!"

"Love you too! I'll get back to you."

She needed him to get onboard to follow the money to see where it would lead them.

However, one of the race-soldiers overheard Amy speaking to her brother, Arthur, at length by telephone about the checks.

In days to come, Chief Campbell started to display some suspicious behavior by holding spontaneous small meetings with Mark. Unexpectedly, there was a change in Amy's work duty detail. Amy got the news when she returned to work the next day.

Chief Campbell informed Amy, "I'm taking you off desk duty starting today."

"What do you mean? I'm being removed from desk duty?"

"Yes! Amy, I need you back out on the streets! You're going out with Officer Chad."

"Officer Chad? He's definitely a strange fruit!"

"He's your fellow officer! And I need you out there!"

"Why the sudden change?"

"I've had a change of heart. You've been on desk duty long enough."

In the meantime, I was spending a tremendous amount of time after work, training and working out counter measures and street tactics for defense purposes and hand-to-hand combat with the street-soldiers. I also trained them on how to disarm a gunman. We continued the weapons training with the money donated by the families that lost loved ones due to the misconduct of those in law enforcement.

When I met with street-soldiers, I told them, "I said that I would get you men guns!"

A street-soldier replied, "Yeah man! We're ready to handle those devils!"

I told them, "Now, you guys know how to handle the weapons. You're very proficient with your guns!"

A street-soldier replied, "That's what I'm talking about! I'm ready for war! We're ready for war!"

I had to make it clear to them.

"You men were always ready for war; you just needed to know who to declare war on!"

A street-soldier replied, "We are ready for change!"

I told them, "Okay men! Let's stay focused! Let's stay ready!"

I managed to get an arsenal of weapons. We were preparing to take on Mark and the race-soldiers because they were looked upon as street-thugs. I had applied to get concealed weapons permits for the street-soldiers, posing as security guards.

Amy felt nothing but repugnance with the idea of working and riding with Mark's friends. On their first day of work, just about two hours before the sun was starting to set, they were dispatched to a report of a 211 in progress at 1024 East Lou Dillon Street. When they arrived, it was in an unincorporated area of Watts, California with old decaying abandoned buildings and vacant lots. There was no sign of assailants; neither were there any victims. Amy, as the passenger partner working the radio, made an attempt to call it in as a false call or prank just as the race-soldier, Officer Chad, insisted on getting out of the squad car to have a look around.

Amy looked around and said, "Well, there's nothing going on here, I'm going to call it in as a code four."

Officer Chad suggested, "No! Not yet. Let's get out and check it!"

Amy felt that it was a waste of time. "There's nothing going on here."

Officer Chad insisted, "Let's check it out! Let's just shine our flashlights and take look inside."

Amy agreed.

"Yeah, okay!"

They entered the abandoned building with only flashlights in hand, as Chad led the way. Once they were inside, Mark arrived at the scene without siren or squad car emergency lights. Mark entered the building with his service revolver in hand as if he were there to assist. However, he was there for a more sinister reason. Amy was so startled she was unable to quickly draw her service revolver. She was paralyzed with fear.

Amy was shocked.

"Hey, Damn! You scared the shit of out me! What are you doing here?"

Mark was pointing his gun.

"Don't move!"

Amy looked surprised.

"What?"

Officer Chad chimed in.

"Yes! Don't move! We will teach you to snoop around!"

Amy yelled out.

"Oh, No! No!"

Mark had a tight grip on her neck.

"Stop resisting! Stop fucking resisting!"

She realized that he was actually pointing his revolver at her head. Then Chad turned around with his revolver and pointed toward Amy's torso. Amy dropped her flashlight and threw her hands up as Mark grabbed her in a chokehold. As he strangled her, she fought back in a struggle while Mark continued to whisper in her ear, "Stop resisting!" He held her in a chokehold until her lifeless body went limp. She met her demise due to strangulation. He released her. She fell to the floor of the foyer of the abandoned building; her body laid there.

Mark told Chad how to make the report.

"Hey, make sure your statement is clear that someone came out of nowhere, and killed her."

Chad agreed.

"I'll be sure not to mention you were ever here. It was just Officer Freeman and I on the scene."

Mark and Chad conspired a story of an unknown assailant coming out of nowhere and ambushing Amy while they were separated, as Chad searched the other locations of the building.

It was a few days following the day of Amy's murder. I closed the world out and still could not get a clear mind. I was so despondent, depressed, and a risk to myself that Chief Campbell insisted that I take some time off work.

Chief Campbell called me into the office.

"Officer Smith, I'm ordering you to take some time off for yourself."

I agreed.

"Thanks Chief, I guess I really need to clear my head."

Chief Campbell assured me that everything was going to be okay.

"Yeah, take all the time you need. We'll cover you around here."

So, that's what I did.

I began to just sit at home with a bottle of Chivas Regal Scotch as my comfort. I was very despondent. I didn't shower, shave, or bathe for days; I was incapacitated until my mother made a desperate effort to pay me a visit. She needed to reach me and make some sense of the whole situation.

My mother was knocking on my door as if she was on the police force! She knocked until I was able to make it to the door. I took a glimpse at my telephone message machine. I had several messages. I opened the door as she sat down and told me to have a seat. As I sat down, she informed me that there was good news relating to Amy's death. I instantly started to wonder what in the hell was she talking about.

My mother told me, "We really know what happened to Amy!"

"What do you mean? "

"There were eyewitnesses to her murder!"

"What?"

"This homeless couple named Leon and Rachael saw the whole thing!"

"How?"

"They were living in the building! They were taking in some shelter by trespassing."

"Who did they say killed her?"

"These two uniformed cops! They think one of them was her partner!"

"What about the other cop?"

"They said he was a big white guy with an orange tan that stood six foot two, with a heavy southern accent and a confederate flag on his right arm. They were watching discreetly."

My mother stated that the couple was willing to come forward and make a written statement about the crime under immunity of trespassing. It was a fortunate moment. As my mother was delivering me the good news, I began to check my telephone messages. There was an urgent message from Amy's brother, Arthur. His message was left on the machine the same day that Amy was murdered, and it was to inform us that Mark and the race-soldiers were not sworn police officers and that they were not even deputized to patrol the streets.

This was Arthur's voice message:

"Hello, hey this message is for Amy. Amy, that guy Mark Koon runs an organization and they're not police officers; they are impersonating officers. They weren't deputized! It looks like they struck up a back room deal to dominate the community. When you get this message give me a call back."

They were not authorized to work as police officers. The pertinent information he gathered in his investigation from the photocopied checks paid to Mark Koon Inc., indicated there was a backroom deal made. I was seething with the idea of revenge. I had so many ideas running through my head to kill those guys. There was also a message from Amy's father, stating that he and a few of the members of his "elite organization," which handled personal situations outside of the law on "personal levels," were on their way to Los Angeles. He booked hotel suites in the airport area.

Chapter 10

The Hands of Lady Justice

By this time, the powder keg had been ignited. Mr. Freeman and his organization were coming to town to extract retribution for Amy's murder. I had to get my head straight and contact some of the street-soldiers to meet with Mr. Freeman at his hotel. We discussed the information that my mother had given me, and the telephone message Arthur had left for me. Mr. Freeman absorbed every little bit of the details that the street-soldiers and I could muster up. The street-soldiers became an ancillary partner to Mr. Freeman's organization. At that point he decided to just take care of Amy and fly her body back home to Birmingham for a nice burial.

The day before Amy's body was to be flown back home, we had a small memorial for her at our meeting building. Arthur flew into Los Angeles with all of the proof and documents to expose the chief, along with Mark and the race-soldiers. He shared all the evidence with the mayor, FBI, and the governor.

Subsequently, Chief Campbell was arrested, along with all of the race-soldiers. They were brought up on charges by the district attorney's office with one count of the California Penal Code Section 187 — murder charge, California Penal Code Section 538d — impersonating an officer, and California Penal Code Section 186.8 — racketeering inside the police department. Chief Campbell was implicated in orchestrating Amy's death, according to Mark Koon's sworn deposition:

"I, Mark Koon, swear by my written statement, that my organization was paid for its services by ex-Chief Campbell."

In the month before the trial, Chief Campbell faced expulsion from the police force. The mayor placed me as Chief of the Los Angeles Police Department.

"Officer Smith, it's my honor to promote you to Chief of Police of the Los Angeles Department."

"Sir, I am honored!"

"On behalf of the city of Los Angeles, we are proud to have you."

My mother, along with the residents in the community, went to the mayor and petitioned for a Civilian Police Commission Review Board.

One of the citizens spoke out.

"We want to see the police prosecuted by the people! We want to see change! We want another way of doing things! If the chief can't clean up the department, then we will get him out!"

The Commission Review Board would have the power to fire the Chief of Police. The commission would be based on the belief that the justice system is designed to correct itself by law. But if it is corrupt and infected by racism, then it is bound to fail. Therefore, starting at the top with the chief, they must fight to reform it in the interest of justice.

The trial began to get underway with Attorney Arthur Freeman ready to skillfully proceed with the case. He completed his due diligence in the work of uncovering the racketeering operation of the ex-Chief of Police Campbell. In the meantime, while Campbell was out on bail, he was not allowed to leave the state. Mark and the race-soldiers remained in custody in downtown Los Angeles at the Twin Towers Correctional Facility.

The day the trial began there was a very large amount of the community present. Television news crews and the newspaper press headed to the downtown Los Angeles Criminal Courthouse. They filled the courtroom to get a glimpse of the administration of deserved punishment by the hands of Lady Justice, as she wore her blindfold.

The community had the highest trust in Attorney Arthur Freeman and his prosecution team. The community would often call them the dream team. Attorney Freeman toiled meticulously in studying the case, for there would be no deferring justice for the people, knowing that his sister, Amy's death, would not be in vain. He knew that he would get only one bite at the apple, and he had to get it right. Moments before entering the courtroom, one of the community pastors asked a group of citizens to join hands as he led them in an agonizing prayer.

"Father God, we come to you with bowed heads and humble hearts, asking you to step in so that we may receive justice! In your name, Amen!"

One of the two bailiffs made an announcement that the court was ready to convene.

Everyone would need to enter and have a seat so that the 12-person jury could come in and be seated. The selected panel of jurors consisted of nine white men and three white women, with one white man as an alternate juror. Leon and Rachael were already seated as witnesses near the front row, right behind the prosecutor's desk.

The bailiff shouted, "All rise!" The judge entered the courtroom from his chambers and took the bench. The criminal defense attorney's team was seated at the counsel table across from Arthur.

The judge spoke to the defense and prosecuting attorneys.

"Is counsel ready?"

Arthur spoke up.

"We're ready, your Honor"

On the other hand, the defense wasn't ready.

"Your Honor, may I have a sidebar?"

The judge seemed aggravated.

"What is it, counsel?"

The defense spoke in a whisper.

"Your Honor, my clients are not all present!'

He responded angrily, "What's happening, counsel?"

The defense pleaded with the judge, "I need a recess, your Honor! I need to reach a client."

As the second bailiff exited a side door of the courtroom to retrieve Mark and the race-soldiers., the defense attorney began to look around to search the room for Campbell to make his appearance for court. One of the defense attorneys stepped out of the courtroom into the hallway to search for Campbell. The search went on for about 30 minutes until the judge began to question the first bailiff as to the whereabouts of the second bailiff. He ordered him to go to the back and assist the second bailiff with the prisoners. When he reached the back room holding cell, he stumbled across the bailiff, lying in the back hallway on the floor, knocked out cold.

The first bailiff began to question the second bailiff.

"Hey man wake up and get up! What happened to you?"

The second bailiff woke up and began to explain.

"All I can remember is walking the prisoners down the hall from the cell!"

He continued to question him for more detail.

"Did you see anyone else?"

The bruised bailiff was trying to collect his bearings.

"No! But I did feel a blow to back of my head!" his partner informed him.

"Well the prisoners are gone now!"

The bailiff was in disbelief.

"What, all of them? Man!"

The first bailiff gave him the awful news.

"Yeah, man! They must have escaped!"

He stated that he reached the holding cell where Mark and six of the race-soldiers were handcuffed and chained to one another. He had them walking down the back hallway in a single file. He was just a few steps away from entering the courtroom, and just as he was passing a storage closet, he was hit and knocked out.

A team of four assailants came from behind him and hit him in the back of the head.

One assailant asked another, "Is he out?"

The assailant assured the other one, "Yeah, he's knocked out!"

Another assailant ordered the others, "Okay, move them out to the back! Get them into the van!"

The assailants gave an order to the race-soldiers.

"Hurry! Hurry!"

Mark was confused and happy and the same time.

"Who are you guys? Why are you helping us?"

One of the assailants shouted out an order in a whisper.

"Shut up! Get into the van! Move it! Move it!"

Mark continued to praise the assailants.

"I'm glad you guys are helping us get away!"

The assailant repeated himself.

"Shut up! Just get in the van!"

Mark felt elated to be evading justice.

"All right! All right! We're moving!"

The prisoners were nowhere to be found in the building. The deputies reviewed the footage from the video surveillance cameras. It was discovered that four extremely huge, masked men in uniform had made their way into the back of the courtroom, waiting for the right moment to make an attack on the bailiff who had the keys. They made their way out of a back door and into an unmarked white Dodge van.

The police dispatch radio was making calls out.

"Calling all units! Calling all units! We have an All Points Bulletin (APB)! Be on the lookout for an all-white Dodge van! License CA 375-AL21! All occupants considered armed and dangerous! Calling all units! Calling all units! Be on the lookout!"

Either the masked men helped prisoners escape or they were abducted. As the manhunt for the prisoners was in progress, the search for Campbell was in progress. Calls were made to Campbell's home until the judge issued a search warrant for Campbell's home. Once the officers made entry into Campbell's home, they found a gruesome image of the slain ex-Chief of Police, suited, dressed for court, face-down, handcuffed, swimming in a pool of his own blood, a gunshot wound to the back of his head, with one of his own service revolvers on the floor. A hand-written note was found on the coffee table that read, "Justified."

A police detective on the scene made out a report.

"We have one deceased Theodore Campbell, murdered with a bullet wound to the back of his head, handcuffed to the back, and a message note that reads 'Justified.'"

Another detective on the scene shouted, "Okay! Okay! Let's call the coroner. Move out! There's nothing to see here!"

The whole city was in an uproar with the news of crooked cops on the run as they escaped from jail. The manhunt was on. They were cautioned to be on the lookout for seven bad ex-cops, and they could be armed and dangerous. News reporters were reporting around the clock as the citizens were locking their doors and windows and staying glued to their televisions.

Chapter 11

No Justice! No Peace!

As the manhunt continued to find the missing prisoners, the escape was being broadcast all over the television news stations. Reporters were scrambling to be the first to get the story of the big escape. The only strange and most sinister thing about the investigation was that during the time of the escape, the masked men did not take the keys to the handcuffs. However, they did strip the bailiff of his gun. Later on that night, the white Dodge van was found. The bodies of all the prisoners were inside the abandoned van, all still handcuffed and shackled to one another at their feet. The detective reported that the deceased apparently suffered from chokehold strangulation while being battered and tortured. Each of the prisoners received a contact gunshot wound to the forehead. He said there was a brutal struggle that indicated lots of resistance before the shot to their heads. There were no fingerprints or any clues of a perpetrator. It was an awful conflict.

Good evening, everyone. This is Alex of Channel 7 news reporting.

"An ex-police officer has been found murdered with his own gun this evening! He was up on charges for racketeering and murder! It looked as if he had gotten dressed to appear in court this morning!

And in more news, the seven escaped or abducted convicts were found deceased near the LAX airport! They were up on charges for impersonating officers among other charges. This is Channel 7 news reporting! Stay tuned!"

These incidents brought the wheels of justice to a screeching halt. The criminal cases of Theodore Campbell, Mark Koon, and the race-solders were all dismissed due to their unforeseen demise. Some of the citizens were upset and dismayed. They didn't understand what happened to the case. They didn't know that if defendants were to die during the proceedings of a case, the case would be dismissed and that would end all the criminal charges against them.

One of the citizens shouted out.

"What do you mean the case is dismissed? I want justice! Justice now!"

Other citizens joined in.

"No justice! No peace! No justice! No peace!"

In the days that followed the dismissal of the case, I had a surprise visit at the department of about 20 members of the community led by my mother. They stormed my office. It was a desperate act from people who had been pushed too far. I was just starting my new position as the Chief of Police

My mother spoke out with the crowd standing behind her.

"We are here to voice our concerns! We are going to disrupt the social order of things around here. The problem that we have is not due to a defect in us, but a defect in this department. This department has a benign neglect for the community. We will not suffer in silence!"

Ms. Benson spoke up after my mother.

"We don't care who's running this department! We are going to do things our way!"

My Uncle Conrad spoke after Ms. Benson.

"We're fighting and voting to abolish The Law Enforcement Officers' Bill of Rights!"

A citizen in the crowd spoke out, "That shit has to go!" followed by another one.

"We won't let anyone stand in our way!"

The Law Enforcement Officers' Bill of Rights (LEOBoR) protects American law enforcement personnel from investigation and prosecution stemming from their conduct while in the scope of their duty. It provides them with privileges unlike normal citizens. The privileges are written into their contracts with the police union.

My mother didn't treat me, the Chief of Police, as her son outside of her home, so when they made their visit, they were there to discuss the relationship and trust between the police and the community. They needed to make clear that the police department worked for the community. So they demanded honesty and accountability from the officers who served the community.

I stood up to defend my position.

"I do understand your concerns! However, give me the chance to get things in order here! We work for the community! Yes, I know that!"

"Yeah! You better damn well know that!"

I made a vow to the community that I would make an earnest effort to restore the faith and trust in the department and establish a good relationship with our citizens in the community.

I spoke to them to assure them they had my word.

"We are going to work for the betterment of the people! We're going to be a community of one!"

I pledged to use my officers to work with the local business owners, churches, and schoolteachers to make the community a place where the citizens could aspire to the ideal of equality and opportunity. I pledged to allow those with the highest aspirations to achieve, therefore becoming a microcosm of America in which this community could come together as one, resulting in justice for everyone.

THE END

Epilogue

The strength of the African American has always amazed me in many ways. Through their experiences of high rates of atrocities and racism, more than any other group in this country, they have stood strong even while in conflict.

Through income inequality and disparities in education, African Americans have been denied full access to the "American dream," as it was written into our Constitution by our founding fathers and has been codified into law. African Americans have to continue to justify their space, which they occupy in this country on a daily basis.

Dear Brothers, do all you can to stand as men, and God will see you through!

Dear Sisters, may God continue to bless you with the strength that carries our communities.

Don't sell your soul; that's all you have.

IN MEMORY OF SOME OF THE PRECIOUS LIVES WE HAVE LOST DUE TO POLICE VIOLENCE:

Calvin Richards, 39, Lynwood, CA, May 27, 1997

Kendrec McDade, 19, Pasadena, CA, March 24, 2012

Rekia Boyd, 22, Chicago, IL, March 21, 2012

Shereese Francis, 30, New York, NY, March 15, 2012

Wendell Allen, 20, New Orleans, LA, March 7, 2012

Nehemiah Dillard, 29, Gainesville, FL, March 5, 2012

Dante Price, 25, Dayton, OH, March 1, 2012

Raymond Allen, 34, Galveston, TX, February 27, 2012

Sgt. Manuel Loggins, Jr., 31, Orange County, CA, February 7, 2012

Ramarley Graham, 18, New York, NY, February 2, 2012

Kenneth Chamberlain, 68, White Plains, NY, November 19, 2011

Alonzo Ashley, 29, Denver, CO, July 18, 2011

Kenneth Harding, 19, San Francisco, CA, July 16, 2011

Raheim Brown, 20, Oakland, CA, January 22, 2011

Reginald Doucet, 25, Los Angeles, CA, January 14, 2011

Derrick Jones, 37, Oakland, CA, November 8, 2010

Danroy Henry, 20, Thornwood, NY, October 17, 2010

Aiyana Jones, 7, Detroit, MI, May 16, 2010

Steven Eugene Washington, 27, Los Angeles, CA, March 20, 2010

Aaron Campbell, 25, Portland, OR January 29, 2010

Kiwane Carrington, 15, Champaign, IL, October 9, 2009

Epilogue

Victor Steen, 17, Pensacola, FL, October 3, 2009

Shem Walker, 49, New York, NY, July 11, 2009

Oscar Grant, 22, Oakland, CA, January 1, 2009

Tarika Wilson, 26, Lima, OH, January 4, 2008

DeAunta Terrel Farrow, 12, West Memphis, AR, July 22, 2007

Sean Bell, 23, New York, NY, November 25, 2006

Henry Glover, 31, New Orleans, LA, September 2, 2005

Ronald Madison, 40, and James Brisette, 17, New Orleans, LA, September 4, 2005

Timothy Stansbury, 19, New York, NY, January 24, 2004

Akai Gurley, 28, Brooklyn, NY, November 20, 2014

Dante Parker, 36, San Bernardino County, CA, August 12, 2014

Eric Garner, 43, New York, NY, July 17, 2014

Ezell Ford, 25, Los Angeles, CA, August 12, 2014

John Crawford III, 22, Beavercreek, OH, August 5, 2014

Jordan Baker, 26, Houston, TX, January 16, 2014

Kajieme Powell, 25, St. Louis, MO, August 19, 2014

Victor White III, 22, Iberia Parish, LA, March 22, 2012

McKenzie Cochran, 25, Southfield, MI, January 28, 2014

Michael Brown, 18, Ferguson, MO, August 9, 2014

Jamarion Robinson, 26, Atlanta, GA, August 5, 2016

MAY OUR WAITING FOR JUSTICE NOT BE IN VAIN

Justified by Law and Conflict

Author's Biographical Sketch

 Spencer Lennard Smith is a native of Los Angeles, California, and has gained a love and passion for the communities in the surrounding areas. As such, he has observed the challenges, disparities, and racial injustices inflicted upon minorities. This is the fuel that has influenced him to focus on storytelling in an amazing, yet graphic manner.

He is a poet and a published author, as well as a husband and father. Spencer L. Smith, an author who can pen words that render many of us speechless.

Connect with me on Facebook:

https://www.facebook.com/profile.php?id=100000224234
213